"Anyone ever tell y   supremely arrogan

"Often. I'm not averse to hearing compliments, Olympia. And nor do I imagine are you. You really are stunning, *querida*."

Up close she was even more exquisite. He couldn't take his eyes off her.

"Save it, Romeo. You may be infamous for your limitless wants and desires, but I'm afraid you've reached your limit with me."

Nicandro might have believed her if he hadn't trailed the back of his index finger down her bare arm excruciatingly slowly and relished the shimmy rustling over her body. Impossible as it was, her infinitesimal gasp and the ghostly pinch of her brow gave him the notion that she hadn't known a simple touch could affect her in such a tremendous way.

"You're scared. Maybe even petrified. Afraid I will prove you wrong? Or fearful you'll enjoy every minute of it?" He was baiting her, but there was one advantage to toying with an intelligent woman: he knew exactly what buttons to push.

"I fear no one. Least of all you."

The 21st Century Gentleman's Club

Where the rich, powerful and passionate come to play!

For years there have been rumors of a secret society,
where only the richest, the most powerful and
the most decadent can embrace their every desire.

Nothing is forbidden in this private world of pleasure.

And when exclusivity is beyond notoriety,
only those who are invited to join ever know its name....

Q Virtus

Now the truth behind the rumors is about
to be revealed!

Find out in:

The Ultimate Playboy

by Maya Blake

July 2014

The Ultimate Seduction

by Dani Collins

August 2014

The Ultimate Revenge

by Victoria Parker

September 2014

Victoria Parker

—

The Ultimate Revenge

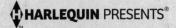

Recycling programs
for this product may
not exist in your area.

ISBN-13: 978-0-373-13278-2

THE ULTIMATE REVENGE

First North American Publication 2014

Copyright © 2014 by Victoria Parker

Printed in U.S.A.

All about the author...
Victoria Parker

VICTORIA PARKER's first love was a dashing heroic fox named Robin Hood. Then came the powerful, suave Mr. Darcy, then Lady Chatterley's rugged lover...and the list goes on. Thinking she must be an unfaithful sort of girl but ever the optimist, she relentlessly pursued her Mr. Literary Right and eventually found him lying between the cool, crisp sheets of a Harlequin® romance. Her obsession was born.

If only real life was just as easy...

Alas, against the advice of her beloved English teacher to cultivate her writer's muse, she chased the corporate dream and acquired various uninspiring job titles *and* a flesh-and-blood hero before she surrendered to that persistent voice and penned her first Harlequin® romance. It turns out creating havoc for feisty heroines and devilish heroes truly *is* the best job in the world.

Victoria now lives out her own happy-ever-after in the northeast of England with her alpha exec and their two children—a masterly charmer in the making and, apparently, the next Disney Princess. Believing sleep is highly overrated, she often writes until 3:00 a.m., ignores the housework (much to her husband's dismay) and still loves nothing more than getting cozy with a romance novel. In her spare time she enjoys dabbling with interior design, discovering far-flung destinations and getting into mischief with her rather wonderful extended family.

Other titles by Victoria Parker available in ebook:

THE WOMAN SENT TO TAME HIM
A REPUTATION TO UPHOLD
PRINCESS IN THE IRON MASK

To my *Q Virtus* compatriots, Maya Blake and Dani Collins. Thank you for the laughs and chats as we concocted and conceived our brave new world. It's been an honor and an absolute pleasure.

And for the fabulous Jennifer Hayward, my CP and best bud. Like Olympia Merisi, you rock!
So this one is for you....

CHAPTER ONE

THEY SAY YOU can't plan a hurricane.

Nicandro Carvalho could. He could wreak havoc with a smile. And after ten years of planning and months of whipping up a storm he was finally ready to unleash chaos.

Zeus. I am coming for you and I will annihilate your world. As you destroyed mine.

The Barattza in Zanzibar, this weekend's ostentatious venue for the quarterly meeting of Q Virtus, was warm, and so muggy his flimsy white shirt clung to his body like a second skin and moisture thrived beneath his mask. Still, he strode ruthlessly through the crush of elite billionaires, intent on his pretty 'Petit Q'—his backstage pass into Zeus's lair, in the form of a five-foot-three brunette in a haute couture red gown designed to attract and blend in equal measure.

Look but don't touch was the cardinal rule.

As if Nicandro had *ever* followed the rules. *'Rules are for boring fools,'* as his mother would say, although her voice was now a distant echo from the past.

Numerous greetings vied for his attention and he offered a succinct nod or a quick 'good evening' and volunteered nothing more. Conversations were like fires—they tended to sputter out if he deprived them of enough air.

His purposeful stride didn't break—hadn't since he'd been Nicandro Santos, a terrified seventeen-year-old boy who'd boarded a cargo ship in Rio to hide in a filthy container bound for New York. It hadn't faltered when he'd concocted a new identity to ensure anonymity from his past life, emerging as one Nicandro Carvalho, who'd sold his pride on the streets of Brooklyn and then wrenched it back by working his fingers raw on construction sites to put some semblance of a roof over his head.

Nor had it swayed when he'd bought his first property, then another, over endless harrowing years, to earn enough money to bring his grandfather from Brazil to be by his side.

An unrelenting purpose and a cut-throat determination that had rewarded him with obscene power and wealth—until he'd been graciously accepted into the covert ranks of Q Virtus, where his sole purpose was to infiltrate and take it down from the inside.

So here he was. And this was only the beginning.

A plan over ten years in the making. Rewriting history to make the Santos Empire—his legacy of a life that had been stolen from him, along with his parents—whole once more.

Nic shut down his thoughts as mercilessly as he did everything else. Otherwise the burning ball of rage that festered and ate away at his insides like a living, breathing entity would surely explode and incinerate everything and everyone in its path.

'Hey, Nic, what's the hurry?'

Narciso's voice shattered his ferocious intent and this time he did turn, to see his friend looking dapper in a tailored tuxedo, *sans* jacket, leaning against the main bar, Scotch glass in hand, the top half of his face shrouded in a gold leaf mask that reminded him of a laurel wreath.

Nic felt the constricting steel band around his chest slacken as a smile played at his mouth. 'All hail, Emperor Narciso. *Dios*, where do they come up with these things?'

'I have no idea, but I'm certainly feeling on top of the world.'

He resisted the urge to roll his eyes. 'Of course you are. How is the ball and chain?'

Narciso grinned at the blatant cynicism, his smile reaching the scalloped edge of gold.

Hideous masks. Requisite to afford them some anonymity, but they only served to aggravate Nic to the extreme—just as everything about Q Virtus did.

A gentlemen's club for the elite. Prestigious. Illustrious. The most sought-after membership in the world. Run by a deceitful, murdering crook.

Ironic, he thought, that grown men, multi-billionaires, would sell their soul to be a member of Q Virtus, virtually handing their business confidences, their reputation, their respect and trust to a common criminal.

Not for much longer. Not after Nic had finished exposing the cold, hard truth and crushed Zeus beneath his almighty foot.

'She's as beautiful as ever. Come, take a spin of the wheel with me. I'd like a quiet word.'

Impatience clawed at him with steel-tipped talons, slashing his insides, but Nic resisted the compulsion to decline outright. It had been too long since he'd seen his friend and he wanted a quiet word of his own.

'Let's grab a private table,' Nic said, not wasting a moment, simply ushering Narciso towards the lavish roulette room and a private table at the back.

Within ten minutes they had drinks in hand and the full attention of a male croupier dressed in red footman's livery. 'Gentlemen, please take your bets.'

Nic tossed a five-thousand-dollar chip haphazardly at the marked numbers adorning the roulette layout and waited for Narciso to make his choice.

'Twenty thousand dollars on black seventeen,' the croupier confirmed impassively.

Nic whistled a huff of air. 'Feeling reckless without your lady present?'

'Feeling lucky. That ball and chain does that to me.'

Yep, his partner in crime was still drugged on a potent cocktail of regular sex and emotion. He just hoped the hangover was a long way off. Nic didn't relish seeing the lights go out in his eyes. Sad, but inevitable.

The wheel spun in a kaleidoscopic blur and he eased back in his seat to afford them a modicum of privacy. With time at a premium and his patience dwindling he jumped right in. If he waited for Narciso to start the conversation he might be there all night.

'Tell me something. Don't you think it's odd that we've never seen a glimpse of QV's Mr Mysterious? Not once.'

Narciso didn't waste time pretending not to know exactly who they were discussing. He simply arched one dark brow and spoke in that rich, affluent tone that had used to fell women faster than a forest fire. 'So the man likes his privacy? Don't we all?'

'There's got to be more to it than that.'

'So suspicious, Carvalho.'

The white ball plopped into black seventeen and a satisfied grunt filled the air. Typical. Served Nic right for not even caring where his chip landed, but right now he had more important thoughts swirling around the vast whirlpool of his mind in ever-narrowing circles. Always leading back to the same thing. *Zeus.*

'Maybe he's not fit for polite society,' Narciso suggested. 'Ever thought of that? Rumour has it the man is associated with the Greek mafia. Maybe he's scarred with a dozen bullet holes. Maybe he's mute. Maybe he's shy. Over the last few months—since the last meeting, in fact—the rumour mill has churned up all kinds of ludicrous tales.'

Oh, he'd heard the rumours. Of course he had. He'd started most of them.

'Doesn't it bother you that Q Virtus could be dirty?' he asked, his voice all innocence with the required edge of concern. 'It obviously bothers some. There are a few members missing this weekend.'

Amazing what a few 'have you heard?' whispers in the right ears could achieve. Doubt was a powerful thing—destructive, flammable—and Nic had lit the torch with a flourish, sat back and watched it spread like wildfire.

Narciso shrugged, as if the thought of being a member of a club that was morally corrupt was water sluicing off a duck's back.

'The club might've had shady beginnings, but even my father and his cronies say the place is clean as a whistle now. You and I personally know several members, and all of them have made billions from mutually beneficial business deals, so I doubt any of it is true. Rumours are generally fairy stories born from petty jealousy or spoken from the mouths of people who have an ulterior motive.'

Very true, that. But the fact that Nic had numerous ulterior motives was something he kept to himself.

'Still, I want to meet him.' What he wanted, he realised, was back-up if something went wrong tonight. If he conveniently disappeared he wanted Narciso to know where he was headed.

'Why? What could you possibly want with Zeus?'

To bring his world crumbling down around his ears. To make him suffer as his parents had—as he had and as his grandfather had.

That old man, whom he loved so dearly, was the only family he had left. The man who'd harangued and railed at him to stand tall, who had propped him up as he'd learned how to walk again when Nic would rather have died in the same bloodbath as his parents.

'Is there something you want to tell me, Nic?'

Yes. The shock of it made him recoil, push back in his seat until he could feel the knotted gold silk poke through his shirt and agitate his skin. Problem being he didn't want

Narciso dragged into the epicentre of a storm of which he was the creator.

'Not particularly.'

Mouth pursed, his friend nodded grudgingly. 'And how do you intend to meet the mysterious, *reclusive,* notorious Zeus?'

Nic tossed back another mouthful of vodka as his gaze flickered to the Petit Q he'd been wooing since he'd arrived the night before. There she was, standing near the doors, unobtrusive as always, yet only a hand-motion away. All it had taken was one look into her heavy-lashed slumberous gaze and he'd thought, *Piece of cake.*

One romantic midnight stroll along the beach and he'd had a thumbprint lifted from her champagne flute. One lingering caress of his hand round her waist and he'd slipped the high-security access card from the folds of her red sheath. What remained was one promise of seduction in her suite that he'd fail to keep and would ensure she was gone from his side.

Narciso followed his line of sight and huffed out a breath. 'Should've known a woman would be involved. I like your style, Carvalho, even if I *do* think that vodka you drink has pickled your brain.'

Nic laughed, riding high on the narcotic mix of anticipation and exhilaration lacing his veins. That was until he looked into his friend's eyes and the mirth died in his throat.

What would Narciso and their buddy Ryzard think of him when Nic whipped the Q Virtus rug from beneath their feet? When he lost them the chance of schmoozing with the world's most powerful men, creating contacts and thriving on the deals that cultivated their already vast wealth. They would understand, wouldn't they? Narciso was the closest thing to a best friend he'd ever had and Ryzard was a good man. Surely he was doing them a favour of sorts—he knew what Zeus was capable of; they hadn't a clue.

'Speaking of rumours,' Narciso murmured, in a tone that made Nic's guts twist into an apprehensive knot. 'I hear Goldsmith made you an offer.'

He practically choked on his vodka. 'How do you know that?'

Narciso looked at him as if he'd sprouted a second head. 'Do you honestly think Goldsmith could keep the possibility of the mighty Nicandro Carvalho, an unequalled dominant force in real estate, becoming his son-in-law a secret for one second? He told my father. Who told me. And I told *him* that Goldsmith is delusional.'

Nic checked an impatient sigh. This was the last thing he wanted to discuss. Except his silence pulled the air taut, pinching Narciso's brow and turning his smart mouth into a scowl.

'Do *not* tell me you are seriously considering marrying Eloisa Goldsmith.'

No. Maybe. 'I am considering it, yes.'

'You've got to be joking, Nic!'

'Keep your voice down! Just because you've been blinded by good sex and emotion—ah, sorry—I mean to say just because you've found e*verlasting bliss*,' he muttered, with no small amount of sarcasm, 'it doesn't mean I want to sign my own death warrant. A business marriage is perfect for me.'

'You're as jaded as I was. Heaven help you if you meet a woman strong enough to smash your kneecaps and drop you at her feet.'

'If that ever happens, my friend, I'll buy you a gold pig.'

Narciso shook his head. 'Eloisa Goldsmith. You're insane.'

'What I am is late for a rendezvous.' He downed the last of his drink as he bolted upright, the lock of his knees thrusting his chair backwards with an emphatic scrape.

'Why would you even consider it? She's a country mouse—you'll be bored within a week.'

Exactly. He could never fall in love with her and he'd have a sweet, gentle, caring woman to be the mother of his children. As to the why—there was only one reason Nic would walk down the aisle at twenty-nine years old. The final goal in his grand slam.

Santos Diamonds.

The business phenomenon that had taken generations to build: his great-grandfather's love affair, his *avô*'s pride and joy, the legacy Goldsmith would only gift to Nic along with his daughter's hand.

He wasn't enamoured of the idea, but he'd promised himself he'd consider it while he whisked up a vengeful hurricane for Zeus to flounder within. So consider it he would. If only for Avô to see Santos Diamonds back where it belonged. It was the least he could do for the old man.

'I will be content. Now, if you'll excuse me, I have an appointment with pleasure.'

The pleasure of the ultimate revenge.

PRIVATE. NO ENTRY.

Blood humming with a lethal combination of exhilaration and eagerness, Nic swiped his nifty keypad over the high-access security panel. While he'd loathed those early days in New York when he'd been lured to the streets of Brooklyn, he'd met some interesting if a smidgeon *degenerate* characters walking on the more dangerous side of life, who had always been willing to teach him a trick or two.

Still, his heart slammed about in his chest like a pinball machine until the fingerprint recognition flashed green and he was standing in Zeus's inner sanctum.

Moroccan-style ironwork lanterns cast eerie shadows down the long corridor and painted the white stucco walls with a brassy wash. The floor was a continuation of the small intricate mosaic that ran through the hotel but here, in Zeus's lair, the colours were richer—deep amber, bronze and heavy gold, as if gilded by Midas's touch. And that touch had embellished every scrolled door handle, finger-plate and urn.

Arched double doors, elaborately carved, encompassed the entire wall at one end of the floor, and as he drew closer faint murmurs slithered beneath the gap like wisps of smoke unfurling to reach his ears. Someone having unpleasant dreams, if he guessed right. Definitely female.

Mistress? Wife? The man was reclusive and malevolent enough to hoard a harem as far as he knew.

Gingerly Nic curled his hand around the gold handle and smirked when the lever gave way under the pressure of his palm. This was just too easy.

Door closed behind him, he stifled a whistle at the vast expanse of opulence.

Ochre walls were punctuated with arched lattice screens, allowing the shimmering light of the ornate candelabra to spin from one room to another and dance over every gilt-edged surface almost provocatively. But it was the heady scent of incense that gave the atmosphere a distinctly sultry feel, heating his blood another few degrees and coaxing his eyes towards the bed.

Mosaic steps led up to a raised dais, at least eight feet square. The entire structure was shrouded by a tented canopy made with the finest gold silk—the weighty drapes closed on all four sides, with only a small gap at the bottom edge. Clearly an invitation to take a peek as far as he was concerned.

Nic slipped off his shoes by the door and stepped closer on sock-clad feet, his pulse thrumming with the devilry of being somewhere he shouldn't and half hoping, half anxious that he'd be caught.

The sudden bolt of lightning that flashed through the room, followed by a sonorous crack of thunder didn't help. His heart leapt to his throat.

Sumptuous cushions and layers upon layers of superfine silk in white and gold embraced the still mound of a woman veiled by the caliginous shadows.

He watched, waiting to ensure she slept on, frowning at the odd sizzle of electricity that ran beneath his skin. If he were the suspicious sort who believed in Brazilian claptrap he'd think his ancestors were trying to tell him to get the hell out of here. *As if.*

Nic shook himself from the bizarre trance and skulked round the rest of the palatial suite, prowling between overstuffed sofas in a rich shade of cocoa, towering fern trees that plumed from barrel-wide bronze urns and the ritzy copper-toned spa tub raised on another dais in the bathing room.

The entire effect was stunning, but it had a homely feel—as if the guest was in fact the owner and he'd decided to give the sheikhs of the Middle East a run for their money.

Finally, in the farthest room, was the answer to his prayers. A wide leather-topped desk strewn with business files and paperwork.

Hope unfurled and he sniffed at the air tentatively, while anxiety curled its wicked tail around his ribcage. Not fear of being caught—more fear of never finding the truth. Never finding what he was looking for. Never coming eye to eye with Zeus himself. Or should he say *Antonio Merisi.*

Ah, yes, Antonio Merisi—aka Zeus. A name that had evaded him for years—as if trying to connect the godlike sacrosanct prominence of Zeus with a flesh and blood human capable of being destroyed was impossible. But Nic had friends in places both high and low, and anything was procurable for a price.

It had been a torturous exercise in patience to discover any other Merisi business interests apart from Q Virtus. Not an easy feat, considering they'd been buried in aliases, but he'd struck gold within weeks and found one or two to set the wheels in motion. Make dents in the man's bank balance. Contaminate his reputation. See how he liked his empire destroyed. As long as Nic got to watch it crumble. To see the very man responsible for his parents' death languish in hell.

Standing behind the desk, he hauled himself up from his pit of rage and resentment and fingered the portfolio at the top of towering pile.

Merpia Inc.

Merpia? The largest commodities trading house in the world.

Eros International.

That one he'd guessed, from the abundance of Greek mythological connotations surrounding the club and a brief mention of the Merisi name in the company portfolio. Consequently he'd plagued the stockmarket with rumours two weeks earlier.

Score one Carvalho.

Ophion—Greek shipping.

Rockman Oil.

Dios…

Multi-billion-pound ventures. Every single one of them. This man wasn't wealthy— he was likely one of the richest men in the world, with millions scattered across a vast financial plain.

The dents Nic had made would be a drop in the ocean.

He battled with an insurgence of disheartenment until another file snagged his eye.

Carvalho?

His hand shot out…then froze when a sharp voice splintered his rage.

'I wouldn't do that, if I were you. Hands up, back away from the table, then do not move a muscle or I'll blow your brains out.'

Busted. Just when things were getting interesting. Still, his lips twisted ruefully at the sound of a husky, sultry feminine voice.

Nic flicked his hands in the air with a high school level

of flippancy to lighten the mood and twisted his torso to spin around.

'Now, now, *querida*, let's not fight—'

The practised snick of the safety catch on a revolver made him rethink. *Fast*. It was a sound that resonated through his brain and threw him back thirteen years. Even his back stiffened, as if he were waiting for the echo of a bullet to penetrate his spine. Rob him of the dreams of his youth. End life as he knew it.

'Stay right where you are. I did *not* give you permission to move.'

A shiver glanced over his flesh at the cool, dominant tone, as if he'd been physically frisked not just verbally spanked.

'As you wish,' he said, taking his voice down an octave or three and coating it in sin. 'Though I'd much rather conduct this meeting face to face. More so if you are as beautiful as your voice.'

Maybe it was her barely audible huff or maybe it was the impatient tap of a stiletto heel on wood but Nic would swear she'd just rolled her eyes.

'Who are you and how did you get into my suite?'

Suddenly the ridiculousness of the situation hit him. Was he actually being controlled by a *woman*?

Shifting on his feet, he made to swivel. 'I'm turning around so we can have this conversation like two adul—'

A sharp sound like a whip cracking rent the air and Nic's jaw dropped as he married the sound of a silenced bullet with the precise hole in the oil painting of a wolf about three feet from his head.

How ironic. *Lobisomem*. Portuguese for werewolf. His Q Virtus moniker.

Omen? He damned well hoped not.

The smell of the gunpowder residue curled through his sinuses and the past seemed to collide with the present, making his stomach clench on a nauseating pang. Sweat trickled down his spine and he had to surreptitiously clear the thickness from his throat just to speak.

'Crack shot, *querida*.' Question was, why wouldn't she let him turn, look at her?

'The best, I assure you. Now, tell me I have your undivided attention and that you will behave.'

Nic had the distinct feeling he wasn't going to win this argument. And that voice… *Dios*, she could read him passages from the most profoundly boring literature in the world and he'd still get sweaty and hard at the sound of her licking those consonants and vowels past her lips.

'I will be on my best behaviour. Scout's honour.'

Not that he'd ever been one. At the suggestion his mother had arched one perfectly plucked, disgusted brow, told him the idea was simply not to be endured and that she'd rather take him to the country club to play poker.

How he'd loved that woman.

Ignoring the misery dragging at his heart, he strived for joviality. 'Though if it's co-operation you're looking for, I'll be far more amenable without a gun trained on my head by an expert marksman.'

'Trouble must follow you if you're familiar with the sounds of a loaded gun. Why does that not surprise me?'

'Guess I'm just that kind of guy.'

'A thief? A criminal? Insane?'

Dios! Why was everyone calling him insane today?

'*Misjudged* was more the word I was thinking of. Or maybe I'm simply enigmatic, like your lover. Or is he your boss?'

'My…*boss*?' she replied, with a haughty edge that said no man would ever lord it over *her*.

He almost rolled *his* eyes then. 'Okay, then, your lover.'

That earned him a disgruntled snicker.

'Think again. And while you're at it who are you talking about? Who is my boss supposed to be? Who are you looking for?'

'Zeus, of course—who else?'

The room hushed into a cacophony of silence; the lack of sound so loud his ears rang. No doubt a pin dropping would have detonated in an explosion of sound.

Nic pounced on the lull—he'd always liked creating a big bang. 'I have a meeting with him here. Tonight. So if you'd like to run along and get him I'd be greatly appreciative.'

A stunned pause gave way to a burst of incredulous laughter. The kind that was infectious. It was rusty—as if she didn't get much practice—but it was out there, all smoky and sultry, and it filled him with a scorching hot kind of pleasure.

Who the devil *was* she?

'A meeting, you say? I think not. And I believe you are toying with the wrong woman, stranger. So forgive me if I just *run along* and leave you with some friends of mine.'

From nowhere three hulks had three guns trained on various parts of his anatomy and he fought the violent urge to cup his crotch. Because 1) despite evidence to the contrary he was of high intellect, and 2) despite their tailored Savile Row attire their eyes were dull from a hard life and the inevitable slide into madness.

Splendid.

For pity's sake, why guns? Why not knives? He hated guns!

'Ah, come now, *querida*, this is hardly fair. Three against one?'

'I wish you the best of luck. If you survive we will meet again.'

He'd always been a lover, not a fighter. Still, living on the streets had taught him more than how to break a lock—which was just as well because he was nowhere near done with this night or this woman.

CHAPTER TWO

SHE SHOULDN'T HAVE LEFT. Walked out. Left them to rid her of the criminal in their midst. Here she'd been expecting news of his disposal to the authorities, or his being shoved onto a plane to Timbuktu, and instead she was standing in the security room faced with three decidedly sheepish guards and a fifty-two-inch plasma screen filled with the image of a prominent, high-profile billionaire tied up in her cellar!

'I don't believe this,' Pia breathed.

Exquisitely tall.

Beautifully dark.

Devastatingly handsome.

And infamous for satisfying his limitless wants and desires. *Not*—as far as she was aware, and she generally knew more than most—renowned for being a felon.

'Nicandro Carvalho. I almost shot Nicandro Carvalho!'

Pia's insides shook like a shaken soda can ready to spray. He'd been in her bedroom. Maybe watched her sleep. She'd been half naked when he'd swaggered into her rooms and for a split second she'd thought her past was catching up with her.

But what really ratcheted up her 'creeped-out' meter was the fact she'd shot her favourite painting. Of a were-wolf. *Lobisomem*. How freaky was that? Considering she'd code-named him herself.

'It would have been his own fault! What was he doing, snooping around in there?'

All three testosterone-dripping men in the room flinched at Jovan's holler but Pia was used to his bark—especially where she was concerned. Protectiveness didn't come close to the way he went on. Ridiculous. You would think she was eight, not twenty-eight.

'More to the point, how did he even *get* in here?' she said, glaring at her supposed security staff, who flushed beneath her scrutiny. 'Find the breach and deal with it. Someone betrayed me today and I want them found.'

Skin visibly paled at her tone. 'Yes, *madame*.'

Purposefully avoiding the image on screen—because every time she looked at Carvalho the lamb she'd eaten for dinner threatened to reappear—she speared Jovan with her displeasure. 'Did you realise who he was before you roughed him up? Tell me you went easy on him.'

'*Easy?*' Jovan said, with a hefty amount of incredulity, and she only had to glance across the room to see why.

One of his men sported a black eye and a broken nose, the other winced with every turn and the third had a pronounced limp.

'The guy should be a cage fighter! I recognised that pretty-boy face within minutes and I *still* wanted to pulverise him, regardless. He could have hurt you, Pia! So what if the man has money? Only last year they discovered that billionaire who had buried thirty-two bodies in his back yard!'

Heaven help her.

'All right—calm down.' If he worked himself up any more he'd either have a seizure or charge back in there to finish Carvalho off. Which would now be a manageable feat, considering he'd tied the stunner to a chair so tightly the ropes were likely cutting off his circulation. 'Like every member, he's been checked out thoroughly.'

Born in Brazil to a lower class family, he'd sailed to New York to make his fortune. The fact he'd come from nothing, was a self-made man, had gained her deepest respect from the start. Pia had first-hand experience of being hungry, feeling worthless, powerless, and she never wanted to revisit *that* hellhole ever again. The amount of determination it would have taken Carvalho to rise from the ashes with no help had fascinated and charmed her in equal measure.

'If there was something amiss about him I would know.' Yet suddenly she wasn't so sure. Her instincts screamed that this man was far more than he'd initially appeared.

'People don't tend to put "serial killer" and "rapist" on their résumé, Pia.'

Valid point.

She tapped at the pounding spot between her brows, feeling as if she'd been given a complex puzzle with half the pieces left out.

'I'm missing something vital. I must be. First he breaks in, then he has a snoop at the files on my desk. Eros longer than most—I'd know that red file anywhere—and then...' She ran her tongue over her top front teeth. 'Now, isn't *that* a coincidence? That Eros International should catch his eye.'

The company had taken a suspiciously abrupt beating on the stockmarket of late. Though in all honesty Eros's share decline had been the least of her concerns. Ugly rumours were abounding, hitting her where it hurt. Her reputation.

Could he be the thorn in her side? The man who'd been making discreet enquiries about Zeus, about the club, about her businesses—the very man who'd been spreading filth and lies?

Maybe. After all, in her world anything was possible. But why?

Stuff it. She had no intention of waiting around while some property magnate ruined her life. *If* he was to blame.

'Turn off the screens. I'm going in there.'

She wanted answers and there was only one way to get them. She just hoped she was wrong and there was some perfectly good explanation for his breaking and entering.

Yeah, right. Call her foolish, but she didn't want Nicandro Carvalho to be at the centre of her current storm.

'*What?*'

'You heard me.'

While Jovan dismissed his men with a quiet word her gaze sought out Nicandro Carvalho once again. Obscenely grateful that her dinner stayed put and she remained apathetic and unflappable. As if the sight of a six-foot-plus Brazilian hunk with a bloodied lip was an everyday occurrence. She was good at that. Projecting absolute calm composure while her stomach revolted at the sight of her *Lobisomem* in a snare.

She rubbed her own upper arms, sore with the faint echoes of pain. She wanted to scream and rail at Jovan for trussing him so tightly. Perhaps she'd tie *him* up until control was lost, handed to another. See how *he* liked it.

'Did you *have* to cut off his blood supply?' she asked, cringeing inwardly at her snippy tone. Not for Jovan's sake. He was more like the bothersome older brother she'd never had, so she didn't bother to pull her punches with him. But the last thing she needed was to come over unhinged to her staff. *'Women are emotional liabilities,'* her father would say. Not her. Not since he'd made her into a living, breathing machine.

'Who cares if I did?' Jovan asked.

Pia cared—for some bizarre reason. But she wasn't about to tell him that. Just as she wasn't about to admit that at times she'd secretly watched Nicandro Carvalho over the past year. There was something darkly arresting about him. One look at his brooding beauty, at that dark skin that looked as if exotic blood ran through his veins, and she felt giddy with it all.

Pia was tall for a woman, and yet his towering height, wide shoulders and the thick biceps bulging from where his arms strained made her feel like a porcelain doll. Though he was snared, anyone could see his bearing was straight, confident, almost regal—like titan warriors and powerful gods. Not an image she would expect from a boy born in the Rio slums. The fact that he took pride in that fact, felt no shame for his poor origins and preferred to acknowledge the truth and stand tall with dignity, had lent him a kind of reverence in her eyes. *She'd* never been able to shake the stigma of it all.

Hung loosely about his face, his hair was the deepest shade of brown. She suspected it would curl when wet, drying into untamed flicks that twisted to his shoulders and fell wantonly about his face. Sharp brooding eyes almost black in their depths were framed lavishly with thick dark lashes: luscious, evocative and dominating.

And there was that word again—*regal*—rolling through her mind as she frantically tried to piece together the *how* and *why* he had broken into her suite and was now trussed to a chair. None of it made sense.

Jovan's hard voice ripped her attention from the seriously ripped Carvalho and she spun to see him leaning his six-foot-five frame against a bank of security screens.

'He did this to himself, Pia. Let me deal with him—please?' His chiselled features twisted, playing out a complex series of emotional shifts.

'No. He wants something.' Right then she flashed back to their brief conversation. 'And I suspect it is something only Zeus can give—otherwise why lie about having a meeting prearranged? So before he destroys my club with his ugly rumours, or costs me another twenty-five million on the stockmarket, I want to know why.'

Jovan grumbled in the way Pia had learned to ignore. 'So what do you intend to do with him?'

Stress and worry lined his brow, reminding her of the day they'd met. When he'd swept her into his arms as she'd lain knocking on death's door outside her father's palatial entryway. Sixteen years old and before then she hadn't even known her father existed. Without Jovan, Pia doubted she would have survived in her father's frigid Siberian world.

'I can't believe I'm saying this, but I have no idea.'

Commodities? A cinch. Juggling multi-million-dollar investments every day? A breeze. Dealing with people? Excruciating torture.

'I'll just have to play it by ear. Question him. Find out what he wants and why.'

Jovan snorted. 'Good luck with that one. He is arrogant. Overly cocky and dangerously determined.'

'Then we are equally matched. I don't believe in coincidences, Jovan. My gut tells me he's responsible for the rumours and the mayhem at Eros, and if so he wants something and won't disappear until he gets it. It would be foolish of me to take my eyes off him for one second.'

'So we put him on watch. Twenty-four-seven.'

'Or I go in there. Deal with him. Quickly. Quietly.'

'Pia, please. It is too risky.'

'Since when have I been afraid of a little risk?' *Never.* Fear would never touch her heart again. 'He's sure to tell me far more than he would ever tell you, and I'll hazard a guess he'll remain obstinate until he meets the man behind Q Virtus anyway.'

'He'll be waiting a long time.'

'Quite. So I'll put him off. Persuade him to deal with me and figure out what he's looking for. Why he'd chance his membership, his reputation, his business and fortune, by toying with the club. With me personally. He must know Zeus could bring him down.'

'But you'll place yourself in jeopardy. Under the spotlight. What if he realises you and Zeus are one and the same person? That your father is dead?'

Without thought Pia let her fingers creep up to her throat, where her pulse beat against her palm in a wild tattoo. Such an outcome wasn't even worth contemplating.

'He won't. He's a man. He's predictable and he won't

look beyond my breasts. Women are designed for whoring or childbearing in his world—the truth wouldn't occur to him in a million years. Granted, very few people know Antonio Merisi had a daughter, but my existence is no secret. If he looked in the right places he'd know I exist. When I tell him he'll think I am merely ornamental—a pampered child—so I doubt he'll crow to his friends that he was wrestled to the ground by a mere female.'

The man had a superb business mind and a vast IQ, but he was arrogant and conceited and as dominant as they came. Any battle between them would likely stay behind doors.

'This is my life we're talking about and the future of a club I swore would stand the test of time.' Damn the old rules. '*Damn* the dinosaurs that litter the ranks of my club.'

They'd never accept leadership from someone with a sullied past such as hers. Not only that, but the gentlemen's club was bound by rules—archaic, chauvinistic rules created by troglodytes—that declared only a Merisi man could lead. Only a man could own and control the largest business interests in the world.

Yet here she was. Groomed. Her path decided the moment her father had seen her, semi-conscious in Jovan's arms. She'd become the son Antonio Merisi had never had. His heir. His corporate assassin. The girl he'd called worthless, tainted, illiterate trash at first glance, making her feel dirtier than the clothes on her back. The same girl who'd then taken his fortune and quadrupled it within the first two years of living under his excessively opulent roof.

She was master of the most exclusive club in the world. Perpetually in hiding. Habitually alone. And that was the way it must stay.

'If my instincts are right he's declared war and I'm fighting blind—ignorant of the cause. If I'm to have any chance of surviving I need the right weapon to wield. Turn off the screens, Jovan.' Her tone brooked no argument. 'I'm going in.'

The monitors flickered to black and a moment later a faint tap on the door preceded Clarissa Knight, one of the Petit Qs, shifting on her feet as she was nudged through the space, a telling flush driving high on her cheekbones.

The pennies dropped more quickly than a Las Vegas slot machine flashing 'Winner' in neon lights.

Oh, wonderful. A lovesick puppy.

Pia checked a disgusted growl. 'Oh, Clarissa, tell me he promised you the world—or at least a permanent position in his bed?'

Simultaneously Clarissa's eyes fell to the floor and Jovan raised a small, flat high-tech sensor pad in the air, his expression warning her not to underestimate their intrepid foe.

Fingerprint recognition.

Her anger dissipated as fast as it came. She wasn't going to ask Clarissa how it felt to be used. She remembered humiliation and worthlessness all too well.

Somewhere in that dark abyss between unconsciousness and lucidity a razor-sharp rapping registered and Nic tried for a gentle head-shake. His temples loathed that idea, twisting his stomach into a tight knot, pleading with him not to even attempt it a second time.

Prising his bruised eye open wasn't much of a picnic either, but his heuristic brain—not to mention his sense of self-preservation—was keen to know exactly how much trouble he was in.

And he *was* in trouble. The ropes cutting into the skin of his wrists was a dead giveaway.

Well, he'd been in worse situations. *Look on the bright side, Nic. You're in. Zeus is here. Somewhere. They haven't thrown you out. Yet.*

Neck aching from being slumped forward, he cautiously raised his head to take in his surroundings.

His mind registered the darkness, the shadows prancing around the bare room, before he focused on a single stream of moonlight shining through the only small window, illuminating one stiletto-heeled foot tap-tap-tapping on the floor.

Ah. He suspected that was the culprit responsible for the lethargic woodpecker hammering at his head. Yet, oddly enough, all was forgotten as his appreciative eyes glissaded upwards.

Vintage towering black patent heels with an inch-thick sole. Sculpted ankles and toned calves. Sheer stockings draping long, long luscious legs and disappearing beneath a short, black figure-hugging pencil skirt.

His mind took another detour, wondering when he'd last had sex. Full-on, hedonistic, mind-blowing, erotic carnality usually kept his body taut, but now he thought about it he hadn't felt the need in months. Little wonder he was famished.

'Good evening, Mr Carvalho.'

A rush of heat shimmered over his skin like a phantom fire. 'Well, well, well—if it isn't my little gunslinger.'

'We meet again. How are you feeling?'

Mouth as dry and hot as the desert sands, he licked his lips. His voice *still* came out gravelly with repressed need. 'Much better for seeing you, *querida*. Or at least the half that I can see. I do wish you'd come a little closer. You can trust me.'

'Said the wolf to the lamb,' she quipped. 'Was it that charming reprobate tongue you used to gain access to my private suite, Mr Carvalho?'

'Call me Nicandro, please. I'd like to think my submissive aspect puts us on first-name terms at least. Right now you could do anything you desired to me.'

Straddling his lap would his first choice. Pressing her

breasts into his chest and licking into his mouth and down the column of his throat would be the second. The agony of feeling her all over his body but being unable to touch… Exquisite torture.

'Very well…*Nicandro.*'

His name rolled deliciously from her mouth with a hint of European inflection. Italian, or maybe Greek. He didn't miss the fact that she still hadn't given him her name, but he was too busy imagining thick, dark curling locks and hazel eyes to match that smoky, sultry voice.

'Let us discuss the misdemeanour of breaking and entering. It stands to reason—our being on first-name terms, after all—that you should tell me exactly what you were doing in my private rooms this evening.'

'Tell me your name and I will.'

That she didn't want to was clear. But two could play this game, and he hadn't needed to hear the safety click of her revolver or the commands she'd issued to the staff to tell him this woman held power. Exactly how much he had yet to figure out.

'My name is Olympia Merisi.'

Now, *that* was unexpected. He barely managed to swallow the sharp hitch in his breath.

'Ah. The little wife, then?' A healthy dose of disappointment made him frown. What did he care *who* she was chained to?

'Little? Now, *there* is something I've never been called. As for me being a wife—angels will dance in hell before I submit to any man.'

Nic could soon change that. In fact he was tempted to make it his mission. Which was incongruous, considering he hadn't even seen her face yet.

'A more accurate description for me would be…*daughter.*'

Everything stopped, as if someone had pressed 'pause' on the drama that was his life.

Zeus had a daughter. Well, now, every cloud had a silver lining and it seemed the fates were looking down on him tonight.

How utterly opportune. How devilishly delicious.

This new information gave him extra verve to break loose and he regained his attempts at loosening the knots binding his wrists as he found his tongue.

'In that case I do hope I didn't cause too much damage to your father's security staff. I was hoping to meet the man himself to apologise.' If he were Pinocchio his nose would have poked her eye out by now.

'That is very decent of you,' she said, skating the lines of sarcasm.

'I thought so too. I'm a very decent man.'

'That remains to be seen. You see, I have the very old-fashioned view that seducing a member of my staff and breaking into private quarters does not decent make.'

He flashed her a mock-aggrieved look. 'Now you are just nitpicking, *querida*. I was curious, that is all.'

A small flat black box spun through the air and landed at his feet with a clatter.

Ah. Busted.

'I would expect to find such high-tech equipment in the hands of a CIA operative, not a man who is merely curious to meet another. I very much doubt you'd find such a thing in the electronics section at the local store.'

Nic shrugged. Forgot he was slightly incapacitated and wrenched his shoulder. *Dios*, it hurt like hell. He was going to get her back for this and he'd enjoy every single second.

What had she said? The local store? He wished. It would have been a damn sight cheaper. 'Let us say I have friends in high places.'

'MI5? The White House?'

'The Bronx.'

She huffed out a genuine laugh and, just as it had earlier, a hot kind of thrilling pleasure infused his blood with a sullen pulse of want. *Come on, Olympia, show me your face. You're beautiful—I know it.*

'Any normal person would've asked for an appointment. Ever heard of a phone?'

'Believe it or not, I much prefer the personal touch—'

'Oh, I believe you,' she interrupted snarkily.

'Maybe curious was too bland a word,' he went on regardless. 'Tenacious?'

'Foolhardy? Reckless?'

He settled on, 'Intrepid.' It sounded better to him.

'Why? What exactly is it you want?'

'An audience with the all-powerful mystery man himself. One hour with your father.'

'Impossible,' she declared, without missing a beat.

There was something no-nonsense about her. She was overtly frank. And, call him a fool, but he believed her. Thinking about it, she didn't seem the type to waste time messing around. As if her time was at a premium.

He pondered that while he doubled-checked. 'He isn't here?'

'No, I'm afraid not. On this occasion the journey was too far for him to travel.'

She had an odd tone to her voice he couldn't fathom, but he still trusted her word. Dangerous? Probably. Considering who her father was. Her father who *wasn't* here.

'Pity.' Or was it? Eventually this woman would lead him directly to Zeus himself, and in the meantime…? The game was afoot and his to master.

A few days or weeks in the company of this woman would be no hardship. He could burrow into her life, find potential weak spots, and seduce her into his bed. Imagine Zeus's horror when he discovered Nic had tasted his precious daughter. It was too delicious an idea to reject outright. It needed serious consideration.

'Is it a private matter, or business?' she enquired.

'Both.'

'Then I'm happy to talk to him on your behalf, or deliver any message you wish. You have my word it will be delivered with the utmost secrecy.'

She began to lean towards him and Nic watched, mesmerised, breath held, pulse thumping frenetically, as she came into view inch by delectable inch. It occurred to him then that she was trying to gain his trust by coming out of the shadows, making eye contact, and figured it was entirely too possible that he was underestimating her.

Nic's eyes strained to focus as she leaned further still, bending that tiny waist, bringing the low, severe slash of her black V-neck shirt into the light, showcasing a deep cleavage of pearly white skin that made his blood hum.

Every blink of his eyes felt lethargic, every punch of his pulse profound, as she came closer…closer—

Dios…

Legs crossed, she sat with her elbow on her bent knee, chin resting on her lightly curled fist; she was the picture of seductive power.

His jaw dropped so fast it almost dented the floor. He felt his IQ dip fifty points. 'You are…' *Stupefyingly beautiful.* 'Blonde.'

Eyes sparkling with amusement, she tipped her head to one side, as if he'd given her a complex mathematical equation and no calculator.

'Ten out of ten, Mr Carvalho. What exactly did you expect?'

'Greek.' It was the only word he could muster. Pathetic, really, considering his reputation. But holy hell and smoke and fire, the woman looked as if she'd just stepped off a film noir set, playing the leading role of *femme fatale*. Visually dominant and unrepentant.

Thick flaxen hair the colour of champagne had been swept back from her face and perfectly pinned in a chic 1950s Grace Kelly look. Then again, the image of Grace Kelly aroused words like *innocent*, *serene*. Whereas Olympia Merisi exuded danger and sin. A woman who would refuse to be defined by any man or to submit to her sexuality. All mysterious and seductive. The type whose charm ensnared a man in the bonds of irresistible desire.

There was no other word for it—her beauty was otherworldly, almost supernatural. Pale flawless skin that shimmered like a pearl, high slashing cheekbones that any supermodel would weep for, huge, ever so slightly slanted violet-blue eyes thickly rimmed with black kohl, and full pouty lips painted in the deepest shade of unvirtuous red.

She should have been called Aphrodite, as undeniably goddess-like as she was. An enchantress able to weave her magical powers, leaving her morally ambiguous. She was danger personified—and didn't *that* just ratchet up his 'want meter' into the stratosphere?

This wasn't a woman you married—hell, no: the very idea was ludicrous. This was a woman you bedded. Found ecstasy in her body over and over, until neither of you could walk, talk or summon the energy to breathe.

Hauling in damp air, he silently prayed for his arousal to subside, wishing he'd felt one zillionth of this visceral attraction for the Petit Q he'd earlier declined.

'Your mother…? Norwegian? Swedish?' With that natural colouring she had to be.

If Nic had blinked he would have missed it. That pained pinch of her mouth, that subtle flinch of her flesh. It didn't take a genius to work out that her mother was a touchy subject.

'French,' she said, in a tone so cold it was a welcome blast of air-con sizzling over his hot, damp skin and leaving goosebumps in its wake.

Nic shrugged. What was a couple of thousand miles? 'European. Close enough.'

Her displeased pout told him to drop it, and even he knew some battles weren't worth fighting. So he did. Well, sort of…

'Please allow me to apologise for waking you earlier, *querida*. Or maybe you should thank me. Your dreams seemed too dark to be pleasant.'

Right there. Ah, yes. She might ooze power and control, but beneath all those chilly layers she was still a woman, swayed by emotions, capable of vulnerability. This was going to be child's play.

'What haunts your sleep, Olympia?' And since when had he ever been interested enough in a woman to care?

'A mere headache.'

Poised and graceful as a ballerina, she stood and pirouetted on her heels, turning her back on him. No doubt to soothe the raw nerve he'd struck. But what really bothered him was the weird, not to mention scary idea that he wanted to take it back, soothe her pain himself.

Instead his eyes followed her like a heat-seeking missile, and he detonated at the sight of the tight curves forming her lush heart-shaped bottom and the perfectly straight black seams splicing down her sheer stockings.

Every thought in his head exploded with the extra blast of heat to his groin.

Holy smoke. She was the sexiest thing he'd ever laid eyes on. He couldn't wait to taste her. To get up close and personal with that stunning hourglass figure. To mould his hands to her flesh, sip at her skin for days. And he would. There was no woman in the world he couldn't beguile and lure into his bed.

After she'd taken a turn around the chair she came to stand in front of him. Up close and personal.

Nic ground his back teeth, scrambling for a reprieve from the sexual tension that choked the air around them and took his hard-on from uncomfortable to agonising.

Turned out the fates had had their eye on the ball the entire time—because if there was one sure-fire way to rid him of lust they'd found it.

Olympia bent slightly at the waist—to look into his eyes

or to endeavour to intimidate him, he wasn't sure and didn't particularly care—and he reckoned he was so far gone he would have begged for her mouth right there and then. *If* a large black diamond teardrop, spectacular and rare, edged with twenty-four brilliant-cut white diamonds totalling fifty-two carats, with a net worth of approximately forty-six point two million dollars, hadn't chosen that precise moment to tumble from the sumptuous lace confection encasing her breasts.

Nic jerked as if that bruiser bodyguard was back with a fist in his guts. One punch and a tsunami of anger and hate and pain threatened to pull him under, drag him into the depths of hell. His chest felt crushed and toxic adrenaline rushed through his body, hardening his wide shoulders, searing down his arms, until he was able to contort his wrists and almost pull free of the ropes. *Just a few seconds more.*

He wanted to rip that platinum chain from around her neck, tear those jewels from the warm cavern of her skin. Just as Zeus's henchman had ripped it from his mother's lifeless body.

O Coracao da Tempestade. The heart of the storm. The Santos diamonds.

He couldn't tear his eyes away. So many memories. So much heartache. So much pain.

Nic had always surmised that Goldsmith owned the jewels, along with the rest of the company. The thought that they'd been separated thoughtlessly, like meaningless pieces of chattel, had broken his heart. He could only presume that when Zeus had sold off Santos he must have kept the diamonds to gift to his pampered daughter like some kind of obscene trophy.

Did she know how her father had come to own them?

A shudder racked his entire body and he broke out in a cold sweat.

Dios, did she know they were smothered in blood?

If she did he would make her life a living hell.

The fist gripping his heart threatened to squeeze the life out of him. It took everything he had to remain calm, not to jump to conclusions or lose the hold on his temper.

Gracefully she straightened before him, and the vigilance narrowing those striking violet eyes told him she was well aware that the *Lobisomem* now sat before her, struggling to stay leashed.

Not any more.

The rope finally fell away from his wrists and it took all his remaining strength to keep hold of the bonds, control his face into an impassive blank slate so she would be none the wiser. Timing was everything, and he hadn't bided his for years only to trip over his anger and fall at the first hurdle.

Nic discreetly cleared his throat and turned his voice to a rich, evocative volume that would diffuse her doubt.

'Apologies, *querida*, my mind wandered. While I appreciate your offer to relay my business to your father, I stand firm. Let us say the topic is of a delicate nature.'

Olympia took another step back and he dug his nails into his palms to stop himself reaching out, gripping her waist, hauling her into his lap, punishing that seductive temptation of a mouth, taking his revenge on her glorious body.

Instead he carried on—as if his heart *wasn't* tearing apart. 'I don't know you well enough to discuss it with you. I'm sure you understand.'

Stalemate. He knew it. She knew it.

Agitation leached from her. 'No' was clearly not a word she was used to hearing.

'Then I can't help you any further, Mr Carvalho. As for this evening—I'm sure *you* understand there has been a breach of trust, and as you're unwilling to explain yourself your membership will be placed under review. I can—'

'However,' he continued, as if she'd never spoken, knowing it would rile her, determined to gain the upper hand, 'if

I had the opportunity to get to know you I might change my mind. Spend a few days with me, *bonita*. I'd love the chance to put things right between us. To prove I'm not so bad after all.'

She crossed her arms over her ample chest and arched one flaxen eyebrow. 'You think me a fool, Mr Carvalho. The way to my father is not via my bed.'

Brainy and beautiful.

'Maybe not, but I guarantee you would enjoy the ride. You're tempted—admit it.'

'As much as I am tempted to skydive from thirty-thousand feet without a parachute.'

He grinned—he couldn't help it. Despite her unfortunate parentage and the bauble now nestled back in her deep cleavage he kind of liked her. Such a shame she wore a harbinger of tragedy around her delicate throat. He wondered then if she truly knew of its origins, because surely no woman in their right mind would wear it if they were well-versed in the omen it carried. The wrath of his ancestors. Strange, he'd never really believed in any of it. Until now. Because clearly Nicandro had been led to it—to her—to wreak his revenge.

He wanted it back. And he would have it. *After* he'd taken her. *After* he'd slid the diamonds from her throat in a slow, erotic seduction she would never forget.

Nic ignored the remnants of his Catholic morality—the stuff that still percolated inside whatever passed for his soul these days—which were suggesting he wasn't being strictly fair, involving her. Odds were she was as crooked as her father.

'I could have you in a heartbeat,' he declared. Exaggeration on his part—she would be hard work. She was feisty and wilful and brimming with self-determination—which would make her final moments of surrender all the more delicious, precious.

'You will never have *me*, Nicandro.'

By the time he'd figured out those were her parting words he was wrestling with a bout of what was surely affront—because the little vixen was halfway to the door.

Nic lurched from the chair and reached the door before she did, slamming his palm flat on the dense block of wood. If she was shocked he'd torn from his hold she covered her surprise quickly enough—simply froze to the spot like an ice sculpture and peered at him the way someone would a cockroach.

'Want to bet?' he said, making his voice smooth, richer than cognac and twice as heady.

A cold front swept over him, pricking his skin through the superfine material of his shirt.

'Anyone ever tell you that you're supremely arrogant?'

'Often. I'm not averse to hearing compliments, Olympia. And nor do I imagine are you. You really are stunning, *querida*.'

Up close she was even more exquisite. He couldn't take his eyes off her.

'Save it, Romeo. You may be infamous for your limitless wants and desires, but I'm afraid you've reached your limit with me.'

He might have believed her if he hadn't trailed the back of his index finger down her bare arm excruciatingly slowly and relished the shimmy rustling over her body. Impossible as it was, her infinitesimal gasp and the ghostly pinch of her brow gave him the notion that she hadn't known a simple touch could affect her in such a tremendous way.

'You're scared. Maybe even petrified. Afraid I will prove you wrong? Or fearful you'll enjoy every minute of it?' He was baiting her, but there was one advantage to toying with an intelligent woman: he knew exactly what buttons to push.

'I fear no one. Least of all you.'

That haughty retort hung in the air, coaxing another smile from him. She was sewn up tighter than a drum.

'Prove it. Spend two weeks in my company. If you win and evade my bed I will desist in my attempts to meet with your father and resign my membership from Q Virtus with no fanfare. You have my word.'

Because her evasion would never, *ever* happen.

Those big violet eyes narrowed on his. 'Together with a full explanation? Because I know there's more to you than meets the eye and far more to this meeting you desire with Zeus. I want to know why.'

It occurred to him then that she must work for her father in some way. Must have come in his place this weekend. She might have already put two and two together and suspect he was at the root of the dissent at the club. Not that she could prove it.

'Of course I'll tell you everything you want to know. However, if you lose, and I take your body as mine, have you at my mercy, you'll arrange a meeting with Zeus and take me to him.'

Two days and she'd succumb. Three at the most.

For long moments she simply stared at him, and it was shocking to admit but he'd have given half of Manhattan to know what she was thinking. He'd never given much credence to the term 'closed book', but this intriguing package was still wrapped in Cellophane.

Finally she gave a heavy sigh, as if she really didn't have much of an alternative. As if he'd pushed her into a corner with his refusal to tell her anything and she had nowhere else to go but to follow him.

What had he said? Child's play.

'All right. Here's the deal. Zeus will be in Paris in eight days. *If* you win, I guarantee you'll meet at a specified time and place. You have my word.'

A smile—so small yet inordinately confident—curved her luscious lips. He wished she'd do it more often—it made his heart trampoline into his throat.

So bold she was, so sanguine, so sure he would fail and she would be the victor. He almost felt sorry for her.

'But when you lose I will have you on your knees, *Nicandro*.'

'*If* I lose I'll go down with pleasure, *Olympia*.'

Eyes locked, they stared at one another. Neither giving an inch. And he'd swear the air sparked with electricity, tiny arrows of fire that bounced from one point of contact to another. One strike of a match and they'd blow sky-high.

'Then you have a deal…*Nic*…'

Welcome to three days of torture.

Even the way she purred his name like that, drawing out the N, made him hard.

'Splendid. And every deal should be sealed, don't you agree?'

Without giving her time to bat an eyelash he slowly lowered his mouth to hers. There was no better place to start the war, and his body begged for just one kiss, one taste.

Gossamer-light, Nic brushed his lips across hers and lavished the corner of her mouth with a lush velvet kiss. Electricity hissed over his skin, his blood seared through his veins on a scream of satisfaction, and before he knew it he stepped closer. Her breasts crushed against his chest and he fingered her sweet waist while he swept his tongue across the seam of her lips, demanding entry, commanding more.

Dizzy, as if she'd put him under some kind of spell, his mind stripped itself clean and he nipped at the plump flesh and sucked gently, desperate to be inside her warm heaven. She tasted of sweet, hot coffee liqueur, and if she'd just let him in…

After a few more seconds he drew back. Frowned.

Passive, emotionless—she hadn't moved one muscle and her skin was like ice, her blood-red lips equally devoid of warmth. Even her violet-blue stare was cold and vacant.

The shock of it made his tone incongruous. 'Olympia,

you are frozen, *querida*.' A coil of serpents in the pit of his stomach couldn't have unsettled him more.

Lifting her chin she gifted him a small smile. Except it wasn't cold—it was sad.

'I *am* frozen…*querido*. Inside and out. Ah, Nicandro, you really have no idea who you are playing with, do you?'

Her hand to the handle now, she hauled the door wide and he floundered for a beat, stepping backwards, his foot crushing the small black sensor pad she'd tossed at him earlier.

The inevitable crack snapped him back to his wits, 'Hold up there, ice queen. The Petit Q. She was innocent in all this. Promise me the girl will—'

'Be removed from the premises. Good evening, Nicandro.'

Next thing he knew she was gone—the razor-sharp tap-tap of her towering heels vibrating in the void around him.

'*You really have no idea who you are playing with, do you?*'

Wasn't that the truth?

CHAPTER THREE

PIA PULLED THE double doors to her suite closed behind her and fought the urge to slump against the carved wood. Bad enough that she raised her fingertips to the corner of her mouth to chase the faint echoes of his kiss, shimmering over her lips like an iridescent butterfly.

Old habits truly did die hard, because for the first time in years she was second-guessing herself—and that really didn't bode well. Suddenly spending time with Nicandro Carvalho seemed like a bad, bad idea. But what alternative did she have? Wait it out until he struck again? God only knew what havoc he'd wreak next, and she could not let that happen. Not in *her* world.

'Pia?'

She jumped clean off the floor, then flushed guiltily like an idiotic schoolgirl who'd just had her first kiss from a long-time crush and her big brother had been spying on her. She didn't want to think how close to the truth that was.

'Where did you come from? I thought you were escorting our nefarious burglar to his suite?'

Jovan watched her warily from where he sat looking incongruous—his large frame stiff and upright—perched on the edge of her delicate gold silk daybed.

'Mission accomplished.'

Oh.

Pia's eyes shuttered at the concern marring his face. He wanted to ask if she was okay but he wouldn't. He didn't like making her feel weak. Emotional. Not when she was supposed to be a machine. But therein lay the problem. Machines didn't tremble with the touch of man's hand, at his finger breezing down her arm. Machines didn't suffer a glitch after a soft evocative kiss from his warm lips. And machines certainly didn't stare into his eyes and feel something close to longing, wishing for the impossible.

For one heart-stopping moment she would have done anything to kiss him back. Anything to feel his scorching heat melt some of the ice inside of her—ice that was so terribly, terribly cold. But Pia knew that surrendering to meaningless brief moments could shower you in a lifetime of regret, and he'd chosen the one route to her bed with a guaranteed outcome of failure and causing her maximum levels of pain.

He was using her. To get to Zeus. To Q Virtus. Ignorant of the fact he'd already been in Zeus's company for most of the evening. If it wasn't so humiliating and didn't exhume such loathsome feelings of worthlessness she would laugh. *Sorry, Nic, I've already learned my lessons in love.* Pia could spot a seduction routine a mile off and erect her barricades with ease.

Being used for the Merisi fame and fortune years ago had thrown her hard-earned self-respect to the wolves—with a little help from her father's constant stream of berating anger during the miserable aftershocks of her affair.

'*Women are weak fools with vulnerable hearts, Olympia. You think he wanted your body? Your mind?*' he'd hollered, as if the idea that any man could desire her for simply being Pia was unfathomable. '*True lust is greed for money and power. Surrender to a man and he will strip you of your fortune and glory and leave you as nothing more than a whore in his bed. Trust no man. Not even me.*'

That her hollow, cold flesh should now answer to the practised tongue of a Don Juan with criminal tendencies who was quite possibly trying to take her down could only be the cruel joke of a universe that despised her.

Now she had to drag him across Europe for the next few days, on a schedule that was impossible to change, trying to delve into the intricacies of his mind while he tried to delve into her knickers.

Not in a million years.

She'd just have to keep her head on straight and her eyes on him. The man could hardly kick up a storm if she was watching over his shoulder, and it would give her plenty of time to unearth what game he was playing and why.

The anxiety of it all—the possibility that she was in danger of having everything she'd worked so hard for taken away—made her feel sick to the stomach. *And that's not the only thing that has you rattled*, a little voice said. She told that voice to hush up.

'You look tired, Pia,' Jovan said.

She was. Bone-deep tired. But machines weren't supposed to get tired. So instead of crawling into bed she tried to pretend that she didn't ache all over, lifted her chin, strode towards her office and got back to business.

'I'm fine. You worry too much.'

That wasn't fair. He cared about her and she would be for ever grateful for that small mercy in her life. It would have all been so easy if there'd been flames of attraction between them, but there wasn't so much as a flicker—never mind the high-voltage current that was still racing through her body from—

No, no, *no*. She was *not* going there.

'Get Laurent from Paris on the phone and tell him I've found him a new concierge. Then ask Clarissa Knight to pack her bags and come to my office. She's wanted to be based near her mother for months and this is the perfect opportunity. With a bit of luck she'll find some fresh eye-candy in days, and Mr Carvalho will be reduced to a distant memory. Just make sure Mr I'm-Sex-Incarnate-and-I-Know-It doesn't see her leave.'

It was far too dangerous to keep her here, bewitched under Carvalho's spell. No doubt he'd promise her the world for more secrets, and if the girl thought Pia was casting her out of a job *and* had convinced herself in love with the Brazilian bad-boy anything was possible.

Even Pia—who'd been vaccinated against the Nicandros of the world—had sensed him drizzling charm all over her as if she were a hot waffle. Clarissa wouldn't have stood a chance. Had he slept with her? Devoured her over and over again? And why *that* imagery made her feel queasy was anyone's guess.

'You are going soft in your old age, Pia,' Jovan said.

The only thing going soft was her breasts.

'I'm not so vain that I can't admit to fault. The girl is far too sheltered to be surrounded by Q Virtus players, some of who are no better than vultures preying on female flesh, but she needed the extra money to send home and I caved.'

While those were the facts it wasn't the entire truth, and she knew it. The truth was Nicandro had used the girl, and it left a bitterly sour taste in Pia's mouth. She was utterly disappointed in him—and that was highly idiotic, because it meant she'd placed him on a pedestal just from what she'd read of him, meant her emotions had been engaged. *Fool.*

'Of course you caved. The girl genuinely needed you. I know you hate to admit it, but you *like* being needed.'

'No, I don't.' Did she?

'Okay, you don't. So, do I have the pleasure of escorting *him* to the airport?' Jovan asked, with no small amount of enthusiastic glee, as he walked towards her desk, where she was standing shuffling papers from one towering pile to another.

The fact she was making a mess to avoid this subject didn't go unnoticed.

Oh, hell, this was not going to go down well.

'No.' And since she didn't have the energy to tell Jovan he'd be escorting them both—together—and then deal with the inevitable fall-out—which was so unlike her it was frightening—she said, 'I'll explain later. Get going or you'll miss Laurent.'

Jovan did a quick U-turn and headed towards the door—and the action popped a memory like some maniacal jack-in-the-box. Nicandro's swift *volte-face*. One minute the consummate charmer, the next a predator. The *lobisomem* she'd seen from the start.

Strange, that all it had taken was one scan of his membership request, one perlustration of his past, one glance at the nebulous depths of his eyes and his moniker had bitten into her brain. *Lobisomem*: werewolf. A survivor despite or perhaps in spite of his origins. A lord of the night. His darkness a phantom entreaty to her soul.

But for several heartbeats in that room there'd been such violent anger in his eyes. A change so swift, so absolute, she'd felt the sharp edges of panic for the first time in years.

Where had it come from, that vitriol mutating his gorgeous whisky-coloured eyes to black pools of hate? Indifference she might have understood—but hate? Such a strong emotion. Made him appear dangerous. Deadly.

At first she'd thought his abrupt one-eighty had something to do with her diamonds—the only gift her father had ever given her, the only time he'd ever shown her he cared. It was the only possession she'd ever truly adored. Yet Nicandro had stared at them with a look of abject horror. It was the *why* that was bugging her. Yes, large black diamonds were extraordinarily rare—hers was one of a kind—but the way he'd gone on you would think it was an evil eye, some kind of black art mumbo-jumbo.

Rubbing at the aching spot between her eyes, she decided it was nigh on impossible to figure him out.

'Jovan, before you go, what's the name of that private investigator we occasionally use?'

He stilled beneath the archway leading back to the main suite and looked over his shoulder at her keenly. 'We have several. Though it's usually Mason, who tows the legal line—or McKay, who has no compulsion about being morally corrupt if given the right incentive.'

Another crook. Wonderful. Bad enough she was hearing rumours of Q Virtus being associated with the Greek mafia. Did she have Mr Carvalho to thank for that one too? She'd thank him, all right. With a swift knee-jerk in his crown jewels.

When she had the proof. *If* it was him.

So foolish, Pia. You're still hoping there's a perfectly reasonable explanation for all this—an explanation that has nothing to do with Nicandro Carvalho, aren't you? She couldn't answer that question and not hate herself.

'That's him—he'll do. McKay. Ask him to look into the history of Santos Diamonds. I don't suppose you remember how and when my father took control of the company, do you?'

Jovan paused. Stared at her with an indecipherable look. He *never* paused.

'Jovan? Did you hear me?' Pia hadn't seen him like this in ages. Almost haunted.

He gave his head a quick shake. 'Yes—sorry…distracted. No, haven't a clue.'

He also never lied to her.

'It's probably nothing, but let's have the information anyway.'

'Not a problem,' he murmured, in a low, hesitant tone that said trouble was coming. The kind of trouble that could rock the very foundations of her life.

She just hoped he was wrong.

As soon as the door closed behind him she dumped the papers on her desk and without thinking of posture, or performing for an audience, she collapsed into the chair and sprawled all over it.

She couldn't remember the last time she'd done this, she realised, head tipped back, staring at the ceiling. It reminded her of being no one—a forgotten girl in a basement room that shook with the heavy metal pounding from above, the acrid scent of drugged hopelessness drifting through the floorboards. The girl with a tainted past and only prospects of a no-good future.

In the next second, as if a ghostly fist had thumped the table, she bolted upright, pin-straight, and opened her laptop, pushing that girl—the girl who no longer existed—from her mind once more.

Nic woke to a warm, richly scented African morning, with a foul disposition from the unfathomable unrequited desire he'd suffered throughout the night and a note pushed beneath his door.

I am leaving at twelve noon and flying to Northern Europe on business. If you still wish to join me be ready at eleven.
Olympia Merisi

Join her? 'I do not think so, *querida*.' Did he look like a lapdog? Next she'd want him to bark.

Dios, he felt vile.

He dismissed the flash of self-honesty that his lack of sleep—when he should have slept like a babe after his major victory at the end of an eight-day quest—was making him too grumpy to think straight, and lurched out of bed with a hot head, ready to yank her into line.

His disgusting mood ruined a perfectly good morning as he showered and said goodbye to Narciso and Ryzard—taking one hell of a ribbing about the slight swelling around his lip, which they presumed was thanks to a ravenous Petit Q—and was led to Pia's private suite.

One of the brutish security guards from the night before

reluctantly let him in, and the fact that he looked a damn sight worse than Nic did, sporting a huge black eye, made him feel remarkably better.

'You're early,' was her greeting when he strode through the door, ready to play hell and inform her that *she* would be travelling with *him*.

He didn't notice her sleek, sophisticated up-do, or her flawless skin, or her kohl-rimmed eyes, or that pouty, provocative red mouth. Nor did he take any interest in the sharp-as-a-blade black business suit hugging her sinuous figure and nipping her waist. Absolutely not.

Her beetcake security guard plonked a case near his feet, no doubt wishing it were his head.

'When did you arrive in Zanzibar?' Nic asked, eyeing the cluttered floor.

'Friday—same as you.'

'You have a lot of luggage for a three-day stay, *bonita*. Did you bring the kitchen sink?' Clearly her father paid her well for being...what? A glorified PA on a power trip? She could, of course, be his only heir. He'd have to kiss that out of her too.

'Not this time. That one is Jovan's,' she said, pointing to the smallest of the designer six-piece set.

'And Jovan is...?' For a terrible moment he suspected he was experiencing a flicker of jealousy.

Dios, he was all over the place. What had she done to him?

'My bodyguard.'

Yeah, right.

'And a friend.'

Sure.

His mother had had lots of so-called 'friends'. He'd actually liked a couple of them. Especially the one who took him to a Brazil game, where he'd met the players, but for the life of him he couldn't remember the guy's name. Which was odd, because he always remembered names—

was good with them. It had used to come in handy when his father would innocently name-drop to catch him out. Anything to avoid the screaming matches that had inevitably followed.

Then he realised it was because he was still staring at Jovan—her *friend*.

It took him a while—what with Othello's green-eyed monster riding his back—but he got there eventually.

'*Que?* No. No way. He is not coming with us. That was *not* the deal.'

'Oh, I'm sorry,' she said, all innocent and light, in cunning contradiction of the devilry in her eyes. 'Zeus insists. You don't want to get on his bad side, do you?'

Nic's temper gauge ratcheted up.

'Fine. But not him. I don't think he likes me.' *And he likes you far too much.*

'How observant you are, Nicandro.'

She lowered her voice to a conspiratorial whisper and leaned forward until he tasted her sweet breath.

'In truth, he'd kick you as soon as look at you. So I suggest you stay on your best behaviour.'

From nowhere he had the impulse to grin, and he let it fly in the most wicked, debauched way imaginable. Naturally he earned himself a nice, slow stunned blink from her gorgeous violet-blues.

Unrequited, my foot.

'Now I get it. He's the modern-day equivalent of a chastity belt.'

She must be worried. Downright petrified of being alone with him.

As if a third wheel would dissuade him. He'd once outrun several of New York's finest after he'd stolen a bagel for breakfast to appease his crippling hunger pangs, so he was damn sure he could lose *this* guy.

The edginess he'd felt the previous night evaporated

at the warmth in her million-dollar satisfied smile as she shrugged one cashmere shoulder. So beautiful. So *his*.

Olympia Merisi wasn't frozen. She only needed the higher heat from a slow burn to melt her resistance. He'd moved too fast, his impatience calling the shots, when he should have known better. He had to stop thinking of her as any other woman and use his brains instead of what was between his legs. Not that he'd ever had the need to switch or polish his technique, but people didn't call him a dynamic powerhouse for nothing.

The reason he'd stormed up here now seemed unimportant. Like a tug of war that wasn't worth landing on his ass for. And he was coming to realise he'd have to pick and choose his battles where this woman was concerned or they'd be at loggerheads for ever and he'd alienate her before he'd even begun. So he'd play along, for now, and slowly but surely gain her trust. When the time was right and he held her in the palm of his hand—*then* he'd take control. She wouldn't know what had hit her.

'Did you want something? You're much too early.'

'No, I simply wanted to see you sooner.' And the hell of it was that was the God's honest truth. Not that he intended to panic about it. His desire was to reach his end game and Miss Merisi was going to take him the scenic route. 'Let's do breakfast. I'm starving.' *For more than food.*

'Pia?' the guy *Jovan* said, in an overly familiar way that said he would move Nic bodily if she gave the word.

Go on, buddy, try it. See how far you get.

'Pia…' Nic repeated, staring into those huge seductive eyes and watching them flare as he rolled the shortened name around his mouth as if he liked the taste of it on his tongue. 'Very pretty.'

He watched her delicate throat convulse. 'You may call me Olympia.'

She sounded so haughty and uptight he wanted to ruffle her feathers.

'I think not. If he can call you Pia why can't I? Unless, of course, Olympia is reserved especially for me. For those fortunate enough to have shared body fluids with you.' He licked his lips to emphasise his point—to remind her that despite her deep freeze he *had* kissed her, and he would kiss her again, and next time she would melt.

Her gasp was so faint only he could hear, but any spectator would have to be blind not to see the pink flush enhancing the perfect sweep of her cheeks.

Oh, yeah, she wanted him, all right.

One look at the way her hands fisted by her sides and he also knew she wanted to thump him.

Score one, Carvalho. Ball in the back of the net.

Though it didn't take long before his smile faltered and a dart of panic sped like an arrow into his gut. Had he seriously just stamped his possessive mark on her? No, impossible. He'd merely been staking his claim for the next eight days. After that she could do whatever she liked and he'd feel neither care nor concern because he'd have exactly what he wanted: Zeus.

She was still glaring at him, her glorious eyes flashing with unconcealed irritation. At second glance he revised that to absolute fury.

'I'm going to have to say no to breakfast, Nicandro,' she hissed hotly. 'With that *none too subtle* reminder I seem to have lost my appetite.'

All this frisky repartee was a serious turn-on. Between her posture and his arousal both of them were as stiff as a board. She seriously needed to loosen up.

Right then it struck him. The key to Pia Merisi. He had to coax the woman to liberation. Unpin that hair, unstrap that dress, unhook that bra, unchain all that control. Unleash all that fire.

Undo her one button at a time.

Reaching up, he stroked the side of his finger down her smooth cheek and felt her vibrate like a tuning fork.

'Ah, *querida*. I think I've just given you a different kind of hunger—that is all.' Then he brushed his thumb over her bottom lip and pressed against it in the guise of a kiss. 'Until later, *tchau*.'

Then—in a satisfying juxtaposition to the night before—he sauntered from the room and left *her* standing there, likely foaming at the mouth, watching his retreating back.

CHAPTER FOUR

PIA KEPT HER head high as she slid gracefully into the leather interior of the luxurious Mercedes waiting outside the private back entrance of the Barattza, still holding on to her temper by the skin of her teeth, frankly amazed that she hadn't followed Nic to his suite and ripped him to shreds.

As she'd watched his retreating back, with an oppressive silence thickening the air around her, she hadn't been able to chance a look at their little audience. She only had to think of how that pow-wow must have looked to her people. Hoping beyond hope that she hadn't just plummeted in their estimation.

Sharing body fluids?

Had he deliberately been trying to belittle her? Undermine her?

Didn't he know how hard she'd had to work to be taken seriously just because she was a woman? Of course he didn't. In his eyes she was probably some stylish Jezebel, playing secretary just to feed out of the troughs of her father's cash, sullied with her own craven self-importance!

She could just imagine what her father would have said if he'd witnessed that overtly sensual display of Nicandro stroking her cheek and thumb-kissing her. Her stomach churned at the mere thought.

'You're a woman—you have to work twice as hard to gain respect. Whoring yourself out will do you no favours, Olympia.'

So at the risk of making the situation look even worse, or blowing her true identity and a plethora of secrets sky-high, she hadn't blown a fuse in front of her staff. No, she'd kept her cool. And it had almost strangled the life out of her. Still was.

When she'd made this deal with him she hadn't expected to face these kinds of problems. How it would look to other people. How she would feel about his opinion of her that her value was only high enough to grace his bed.

It stung.

It was a poisonous battle between her hard-won pride and the need to protect Q Virtus.

Dammit, she wanted him to take her seriously. To know she was a successful woman in her own right. Then maybe he wouldn't treat her like some two-bit tramp.

Tough. She was just going to have to swallow it and suffer.

It would have been so much easier if she could have cancelled this business trip to Northern Europe but the time of year was imperative. Winter was setting in and the window for her hotel rebuild was so small she had no wriggle room.

Fact was he was bound to discover some of her interests over the next few days. It was inevitable.

Well, she'd just have to play the pretty little heiress, helping Daddy to uphold the ranks as she judiciously scrutinised her every discerning word.

Or, better yet, not talk to him at all. *If* he ever got his gorgeous taut backside inside this car. Clearly his time-keeping was as abysmal as his integrity.

Briefcase to the floor, table down in front of her, she flipped up the lid on her laptop and scanned the trading page to check the stockmarkets. Her every action pre-programmed into her psyche. Her body on autopilot, going through the motions like the machine she was.

Until from the corner of her eye she saw the man himself stroll from the hotel as if they had all the time in the world.

It was that insolent swagger that revved her temper—the very temper that had been idling for hours—into first gear.

As if there were a glitch in her system Pia's fingers mashed the keys, and no matter how hard she tried to reboot, despite every firewall in her arsenal, she felt as if she was being infected with a virus. The Carvalho Virus. It even sounded deadly.

Case in point: she was now staring out of the window, watching that hateful, sublime, ripped body saunter towards the car beneath the bright flood of the African sun, dressed in suit trousers and a fine tailored black shirt that clung to his wide sculpted chest as the breeze licked over him, his jacket hanging from the finger curled like a hook over his shoulder.

Her stomach did a languorous, wanton roll that utterly appalled her.

There he was—a study in contrasts. With that imposing regal bearing and yet the dissipated air of a roguish bad-boy, with unkempt hair, huge designer sunglasses and voguish shoes. The heady mix collided to make some kind of prince of darkness.

Pia could count her past lovers with very few digits and little enthusiasm, but she instinctively knew what sex with Nicandro would be like—carnal, dark, and completely hedonistic—not her kind of thing at all. Which likely made her dead or a liar.

The door swung open and he slipped onto the leather bench, all smooth elegance as he made himself comfortable beside her. He smelled fresh from the shower and splashed with a hint of expensive cologne that prodded her hormones to sit up and take notice. She ignored them—and him—while her temper shifted into third gear. Lord, she had to calm down before she exploded.

Thinking about it, she always strove to remain on an even keel—her temper having been verbally beaten out of her years ago, when her father's patience had fizzled out and Pia had recognised her snippy tongue for what it was: fear that he wouldn't keep her. But even before that she'd never felt like this. So mad she was flushed with red-hot heat as if she were burning up. Even her clothes felt too tight, compressing her chest like a steel band that suffocated her from the inside.

So by the time the car rolled out of the hotel grounds she was raring to go, her body slamming her temper into fifth gear.

Breathe—for pity's sake, breathe.

'*Boa tarde, Pia.* Where are we headed on this beautiful afternoon?'

One roll of her name around his mouth, one perfectly innocuous question in that deep luscious voice that seemed to brush dark velvet across her nerve-endings, and just like that she lost it.

Pia whipped around to face him. 'How…how *dare* you?'

His dark brows came together in a deep frown but he said nothing, just glanced around the leather interior as if the answer to her fury lay in the cup-holders or the magazine pouch.

'Have I missed something?'

'Only your integrity, your decency and your brain—and that's just the beginning!'

After a pensive scratch of his jaw, he settled his sharp gaze on her laptop and she could just imagine what he was thinking. That she'd found some proof of his villainy to stick on him. Oh, she wished she had!

'I think this conversation would go much better if you told me the precise problem, *querida.*'

'The problem, *Nicandro*, is you belittling me in front of my staff! The problem is you making me feel three inches tall. How dare you bring up last night—a kiss that I didn't want or reciprocate in any way—in front of the very people I have worked hard to gain respect from? You know fine well that *sharing body fluids* could imply far more than a kiss and, considering you'd just broken into my private suite, how did that look? It made me look like a worthless whore with no self-respect, that's what!'

His eyebrows shot skyward. Then the mouth that had invaded her dreams curved in devilish amusement and he flicked those whisky-coloured eyes sparkling with striations of gold her way.

'You are not serious?'

He thought she was *joking*?

After she'd glared at him for a few seconds he finally got the message. 'You are perfectly serious. A *whore*?'

That was what her father would have said, wouldn't he? 'Yes, a whore. Why? Why would you do that to me?'

Glancing away, he flushed hotly, distinctly uncomfortable, and she wished to God she knew why.

'Did I dent your ego so badly it was payback?' she jeered.

'No. Absolutely not,' he said with the force of a gale.

His sincerity almost blew her away.

'I didn't think it would affect you in that way. I was…'

'What?'

He wouldn't say, but his embarrassment was acute and… well, those carved, tanned cheekbones slashed with red made her insides go a bit gooey. Whatever it was, it obviously bothered him.

In the awkward silence that followed she shifted around in her seat, not sure of her next move. Because from his point of view he didn't know who she really was.

This was why her temper was the enemy.

So in the end she let it go. The reason being, she assured herself, to get back on her even keel and wrestle back some control. Because honestly she was starting to act a little crazy. Unravelling like a tatty jumper wasn't like her at all.

'Just don't do that to me again. All right? The deal between you and I is private. I've worked too hard for my respect and it's important to me, okay?'

Shrewd—that was surely the only word to describe his expression.

'So you *do* work for your father, then?'

No, I damn well don't!

'Yes. Women *are* capable of such things, Nic. What are you? Primordial? Anti-feminist? Or just plain chauvinist? I dress well, I live well, and so you assume I freeload off my father by shuffling his papers?'

He had the good grace to look abashed. 'I think I've found one of your hot buttons.'

'How astute you are.'

'And not the one I was looking for.'

Pia threw up her arms with exasperated flair. 'And there you go again! *Must* you look at me and think sex?'

'I think I must. But come on! Give me a break. *Look* at you!' He gestured at her with his hands, as if that helped his argument. 'And, to be fair, I seem to remember thinking you radiated power. It was clear you held some. So there—see? You really must stop thinking the worst of me.'

She coughed out an incredulous laugh. 'Like *that* is ever going to happen.'

Now he threw *his* arms in the air, but his were longer, and far stronger, and the loud smack of his hand bashing off the window reverberated through the car.

'I can't win!' he growled, and followed it up with a blue streak of unintelligible curses as he flung himself back against the seat.

'As soon as you realise that, the better!' she sneered.

As for Pia—she actually felt much better. Sort of cleansed. Who knew that having an argument and not keeping everything bottled up inside her could feel so good? It was a revelation.

When Romeo seemed to find his calming centre again—which didn't take long, so she figured he shared her quick hot temper—he twisted to face her, and ended up doing a double-take at her small smile.

'I suppose you could say I've known many "pampered princesses" very well, but you are right, I'm sorry. I was stereotyping and didn't think it through and that was very bad of me. Forgiven?'

He sounded like a little boy right then. Pia would bet he'd been loved beyond reason, despite his family's lack of fortune, and the remnants of her ugly mood dissolved, morphing into a puddle of envy.

'Forgiven.'

'Good,' he said, looking back out of the window at the tropical white sandy beach as opposed to the lush plantations on her side of the car.

He seemed miles away, pensive, so when he reached over and lightly brushed Pia's knee with the very tips of his fingers she wondered if he realised he was doing it. Back and forth he went, the tickling sensation on her sheer stocking making her tremble.

'Please move your hand. Are you always so liberal with your touch?'

Just as she'd thought, he glanced at his hand quizzically as he slipped it from her leg. Heaven help her—she wanted it back.

He shrugged, flexing his wide shoulders. 'Brazilians are very affectionate people, *querida*. We think nothing of gushing about what is beautiful, or *lindo maravilhoso*, or expressing fondness with a hug or a kiss. Aren't you Greeks used to lavish displays of affection? Or did you grow up in France with your mother?'

Pia kept quiet. There were always exceptions to the rule, and the very idea of thinking about her mother made horror swarm through her veins.

Seconds later she found herself tapping away at her laptop.

'What is so fascinating that you'd rather do that than talk to me?'

She shook her head at him. 'My, my—you have an exceedingly high opinion of yourself.'

He gave her an insolent shrug that said his ego was well founded and she was telling him nothing he hadn't heard before.

'I'm working. Don't *you* have work to do? A real estate empire to run?'

'Not right now. I'm one of those people who can't read as a passenger—the headaches and sickness linger for hours.'

Her fingers paused on the keypad at that statement—the first honest words to pass his mouth and a tiny insight into the real Nicandro Carvalho that gave her a ridiculous little thrill. How pathetic was that? Then again, she'd always been intrigued by him. Much to her dismay.

'You can get pills for things like that. Anti-sickness. I'm exactly the same.'

He murmured in agreement, sounding distracted, and Pia glanced up, hopelessly drawn to the tanned column of his throat, the pulse she could see flickering as he undid the top buttons of his shirt. He must be hot, she thought, because she could feel the heat rolling off him. Hot and ripped enough to make her stomach flip-flop and her lower abdomen clench.

He was just so horridly handsome. So many angles made up his beautiful face, from the prominent bones of his cheeks to the slash of his jaw. Even his mouth was chiselled, almost carved, with that exaggerated cupid's bow punctuating his frown as he read.

'Is that Merpia?' he asked, tilting his head farther to one side for a better look at her screen.

Pia snapped out of her drooling stasis, thoroughly disgusted in herself, and threw him a baleful look. 'You have a filthy habit of snooping, Nicandro.'

He cocked one dark brow. 'Right now, I promise you I'm not being nosy—I am genuinely interested. You have an obsessive compulsion to get back to that…whatever you are doing and I'm itching to know why.'

'God, you're insufferable.'

Truly, she didn't like talking about work, and it had nothing to do with secrecy or her need for privacy. It was the turmoil she felt. Like living on a knife-edge. Sometimes she woke in a cold sweat, thinking that her father had been wrong and she really couldn't do it all—would somehow fail to juggle the million balls that were thrown at her what seemed like every minute of every day. That one of these days she'd be exposed as the illiterate nobody she was—not the mathematical prodigy and business whiz her father had excitedly claimed her to be not eight months after she'd landed at his door.

I devote my entire life to a thousand jobs I never really wanted...would never have chosen if I'd been free.

The sudden vehemence of her thoughts shocked her to the core and made her feel ashamed. Every time she thought that way she felt hideously selfish. She'd been given a new life—a second chance—something many people would sell their soul for. She should be more grateful. She *was* insanely grateful. Yet sometimes she just wished the merry-go-round would stop, so she could breathe if only for a little while.

Nicandro was watching her with a quiet intensity that made her uneasy—as well as grateful that he couldn't read minds. Still, thinking about it, he'd already seen the Merpia files on her desk. It was unrealistic to think he wouldn't see things, hear things and discover things about the Merisi business during their time together. She should draft some kind of non-disclosure agreement asap.

With a drawn-out sigh she spun the laptop around so he could see the full screen.

'Merpia. *Pia. Dios, com certeza!* Of course. He named it after you. You run it for him?'

She gritted her teeth together and prayed for poise and some semblance of self-control. Merpia was her baby. Her pride and joy. Her first true personal accomplishment, started when she'd been twenty-six years old. The one thing she was truly proud of.

'You could say that,' she bit out.

Those gorgeous eyes grew wide as he whistled in awe. And, though it wasn't directed at her *per se*, pleasure flooded through her in a warm rush. It had been four years since Antonio Merisi had been lowered into the ground, and she still hadn't managed to outgrow her need for approval. That she was basking in it now from the wolf sniffing around her life was disturbing to say the least.

'Rumour has it—'

She snatched at the opening like a life-preserver. 'You shouldn't believe or partake in rumours, Nicandro,' she said irritably. 'Very dangerous business. Are you a propaganda man?'

The look he gave her held a hefty amount of lethal softness and it was a timely reminder of what he was capable of.

'There is an element of truth behind every rumour, *querida*. Of that I am certain.'

There they were once again, dancing around the subject of Zeus and Q Virtus and rumours and lies. Neither of them giving anything away; they just stared at one another, locked in some kind of battle of wills, the stifling air between them as high-octane as always.

What was he saying? That every rumour that had been spread was partly true? That Merisi was Greek mafia? That Zeus was a dirty dealer? A crook not to be trusted? If Nicandro was the source he couldn't possibly have proof of any of that.

'Case in point,' he continued, his voice still sharp as a blade. 'Merpia. Rumour has it the *man* currently behind the commodity mask is a genius, with the work ethic of a machine.'

'Really?' she said, as if that particular flash was news to her. 'I would argue it was more a combination of hard work, a dash of good luck and superb instincts. My instincts rarely let me down, Nic. May I call you Nic?'

For some reason the familiarity of him calling her Pia had left her feeling strangely unbalanced in the power stakes, and it wouldn't do any harm to unleash *her* charm and knock *him* off his stilts a time or two.

His ruthless dominance instantly mellowed. 'Of course, *bonita*,' he said as he reached up and brushed a lock of hair from her brow. The gesture was so tender it made her ache.

Careful, Pia, he's playing you.

'So what do your instincts tell you about me, Pia?'

'That you're an extremely dangerous man and I would do well to barricade my bedroom door at night.'

While he leaned closer she edged farther back, until she found herself plastered to the leather seat, his weight crushing against her side, making it hard to take a breath.

'One day you'll leave it open and unlocked, just for me. One day you'll beg for my mouth on yours. One day you'll melt…only for me.'

Considering the heat pouring off him, she wouldn't be surprised. *Please don't kiss me again. I have nowhere to run this time and I'm not sure I'll be able to resist.*

He sank one hand into her hair and the graze of his fingertips against her scalp made her tremble.

Pia scrambled around her fuzzy brain for something curt to say. 'You're going to mess up my hair, Nic.' *What?* That was the best she could do?

A little closer and he nuzzled up to her jawline until her eyes felt heavy and fluttery and her heart leapt to her throat.

With one tiny kiss at the sensitive skin beneath her ear, he whispered, 'One day. Very soon.'

Then he was gone. Taking away his heat and that delicious scent she could practically taste. Lounging back in his seat with all the debauched lethargy of a satisfied wolf.

'So where are we headed? You mentioned Northern Europe? England?'

Considering she was in the same spot he'd left her in, mentally and physically, the abrupt change in topic threw her sideways.

'Headed?'

He grinned evilly, flashing his teeth as if he knew *exactly* what he was doing to her. '*Sim, querida*. Where are we going, this fine and beautiful day? Where are you taking me? Where will I have the pleasure of spending time with you?'

Oh, he was good. She'd thought Ethan was supremely adroit, with the most artful tongue on the planet, but he had nothing on this guy.

Worse still, for a minuscule moment some secret place inside her longed for every seductive murmur to be the truth. Hopelessly wished he wanted to spend time with her for no other reason than that she was a woman he genuinely admired and liked—wanted to get to know. *Foolish, foolish Pia.*

She'd do well to remember that every word he spoke, every move he made, had a dubious agenda. That she was protecting not only Q Virtus but her entire life.

'Not England, no,' she said, pulling herself together, mentally re-erecting her shields. 'Finnmark. Norway. The northernmost part of continental Europe.'

'*What?*' His head jerked upright, eyes wide, horrified. 'Why the devil would anyone choose to go that far north this time of year?'

She didn't tell him it was the most beautiful place on earth, where the air was so crisp and clean it cleansed the filth of a multitude of cities and a dirty past. Nor did she tell him that she hoped it would numb the sensations he wrought in her, turn down the heat that continually flared between them.

All she said was, 'You'll see.'

CHAPTER FIVE

'WELCOME TO THE Ice Castle.'

Nic opened his bleary eyes at the first words Pia had spoken since they'd left Zanzibar and focused on a staggering feat of architecture, auroral beneath the bluish twilight. A hotel made of ice.

He shivered just looking at it.

'Why would anyone in their right mind wish to vacation in extreme Norway?' he said, his tone one of utter disbelief.

Truth be told, there was a part of him still amazed that he'd followed her here and not whisked her away to some tropical desert island where privacy was gratis and he had a cornucopia of heat at his disposal.

Now look where they were. Ice, snow, ice and more ice. As far as the eye could see. Then again, didn't they have sensual thick furs and warm cabins with blazing, crackling fires in these places? Perfect for seduction.

'Why *not* vacation here?'

'Isn't the persecution of minus fifteen degrees enough?'

Dios, he loathed the cold. It reminded him of being close to dead. Those long, endless minutes when he'd watched the life drain out of his parents. Waiting, praying for the pain to stop.

'It's Finnmark, not Antarctica. It's slightly warmer—even more so inside.'

Nic noticed she said this while pulling a thick cream wool hat over her head and shoving her fingers into mitts.

By rights she should look like a twenty-year-old snow bunny, off to the Alps for a jaunt—but, oh, no, with a deft grip she kept a tight hold on the leash of her stylish sophistication.

The doors of the rough-terrain four-by-four opened and she swung her legs around gracefully and flowed from the car. Nic followed seconds later, the chill pervading his bones and numbing his blood. A violent shudder made his breath puff in front of his face in a voluminous white cloud.

'Warmer, you say? For polar bears maybe.'

'I think you'll find polar bears prefer the Arctic Circle.'

The way she said it reminded him of his buttoned-up high school teacher. The one who'd finally lost her patience with him in the art cupboard.

'I was being facetious,' he said.

'Ah, yes. Another one of your less admirable traits.'

He grinned at her over the car bonnet. 'I really shouldn't like you so much. It's asking for trouble.'

Wasn't that the truth? In the end he'd been grateful for the cold shoulder since Africa. It had given him a chance to regroup and remind himself what he was doing in the company of Zeus's daughter and why. When he took her to his bed he had to stay detached, and by God he would. So that meant no drowning in those big violet-blue eyes and no inhaling the scent of her neck as if it was nectar of the gods.

'Trouble seems to be something you are exceptionally good at.'

Nic swaggered round the front of the car, leaned in and murmured. 'Oh I'm good at lots of things. Especially heat, ice queen. Speaking of which—is this your natural habitat? Is a lion going to prowl from my wardrobe tonight?'

She nudged him away from her. 'Only if you get high enough. There's a bar on the north side that only sells vodka. Your kind of place.'

Obviously she knew more about him than he did about her. Or at least she thought she did.

'Do you watch me, Pia? When you help with Q Virtus?' Clearly she'd been sent to Zanzibar in her father's stead, and he wondered how many other meetings she'd attended. Exactly how hands-on she was.

Pia flushed a little and turned to stare determinedly at the forest of towering pine and Siberian spruce that he'd only just noticed. The silvery twilight enhanced the sweep of her cheek, the flawless pearl shimmer of her skin. He couldn't take his eyes from her—was conscious of every breath she drew, the way her full breasts rose and fell, the tiny sigh of exhalation.

'At times I have to watch everyone; don't take it personally.'

'*Have* to?' he asked, and the question made her flinch— as if she'd said something she shouldn't have. 'So you help to run Q Virtus as well as Merpia?'

Not forgetting this hotel and whatever other companies besides. He wasn't sure why he was coming over so incredulous. It wasn't as if a man couldn't manage—why not her? *Because deep down, despite the signs of power, you thought she was salad dressing. The pampered daughter of a powerful man, with a healthy ego to boot, who helps out around the office looking pretty.*

That he was comparing her to his mother bothered him. An heiress who did the bare minimum in the boardroom to reach the country club by noon. But Pia seemed to take it far more seriously than that. She hadn't stopped working for five seconds since they'd left Zanzibar; her phone continually bonged with mail, or texts, or calls from some nameless face she spoke proficiently to with that icy cool composure that simultaneously made him shiver and want to divulge her of her clothing to warm her up.

He'd underestimated her, and for a second he wondered what else he was missing. Wondered if his certainty that she would quickly tumble into his bed wasn't a product of arrogant folly.

Pia smiled wryly, as if she knew exactly what he was thinking. He didn't like being transparent. It boded ill. The only way he'd get through the next few days was to be as mysterious as her father and say nothing that would jeopardise their meeting in Paris.

'Q Virtus takes up some of my time, yes,' she said, as if choosing her words carefully.

And with the past swimming round his head like sharks intent on their prey it was on the tip of his tongue to say, *It won't when I'm finished, so I hope you have a career-change*, but she'd switched gear so quickly he reckoned he'd have whiplash by morning. Which was just as well. Because it occurred to him that the voice of his conscience was getting louder, demanding to be heard. Soon he'd be forced to listen to the repercussions of crushing Pia's world, along with her father. And he didn't want to hear it—didn't want to know.

'You have two choices of sleeping arrangements.'

'I thought you'd never ask, *querida*. Show me the way.'

She shook her head, as if despairing of an incorrigible boy. 'Either one of the cabins, or inside the hotel on an ice bed. Whichever you choose it will be hiking distance from my room, I assure you.'

Ice bed? Like hell. 'But who will keep me warm?' he asked, lending his voice a seductive lilt that promised sinful debauchery.

Nic told himself the tremor that rustled over her was thanks to him and not to the abysmal temperatures in this godforsaken place. He had to snatch encouragement where he could.

'I'll send a member of staff with extra blankets—and before the thought even enters your head, Carvalho, the staff are strictly off-limits here. Please spare me the headache of getting rid of another girl.'

That was another thing. He didn't like the reminder that he was responsible for getting a Petit Q fired. He'd been on the phone all morning, trying to find her, all to no avail. It was as if she'd disappeared like a spectre into the night. It made him distinctly uneasy.

'What's the matter, Nic?' she asked sweetly—a striking contradiction to the inscrutable fire in her kohl-rimmed eyes. 'Worried about your little friend?'

Dios, he was becoming as transparent as glass. But he lavished himself with the theory that she was jealous and used the opening for what it was. *Perfect*.

'Maybe all the rumours of you Merisis being Greek mafia make people suspicious?'

She let loose a humourless laugh. 'What colourful imaginations people have. I promise you, the Merisis have never had any association with the mafia, and when I find out who started that uproar he'll have to answer to me.'

'Not to Zeus?'

'Oh, absolutely. Zeus too. And if you think *I'm* scary you've seen nothing yet.'

'Scary? You are a pussycat, *bonita*.'

'Keep pushing and you'll feel my claws,' she grated out.

Nic grinned. 'Promises, promises…'

The main doors opened before them and Pia's countenance shifted, lighting up like a child on Christmas morning. Such elation, such a beautiful sight. It made something unfurl in the space behind his ribs and flap like the wings of a bird. *Weird*.

Arched tunnels were held aloft by ice columns currently being sculpted by artists with chisels and picks. In the next room ice chairs were being carved into throne-like works of art. In fact the actual artwork was so stunningly intricate the time it must have taken to create the place had to be astounding.

Pia was talking away with a luminous light in her eyes that was just as breath-stealing. 'The walls, fixtures, fittings, even the drinking glasses are made entirely of ice or compacted snow and held together with snice. Which I suppose would be your equivalent of mortar.'

'You love this place, don't you?' he asked.

Splaying her fingers, she glossed over a smooth ice table. 'I like art, and this place is a year-round art project. I like to see it planned and built, the ice chiselled and shaped. I love the fresh crisp air. I can finally breathe in purity rather than the fumes of a car or a jet. This place is magical to me. When it melts in spring I always feel sad, but when it's rebuilt, given another chance to come to life and give joy, I feel…' Her smooth, delicate throat convulsed. '*It* feels reborn.'

Nic almost lost his footing on the discarded shards of ice block scattered over the ground.

Mesmerising was the only word he could think of when she talked that way. Candidly, yet almost dazed. As if she was miles away. He'd hazard a guess she'd forgotten who she was talking to. But Nic hadn't missed the way she'd hitched on her words and spoken as if she'd seen so much darkness and ugliness in her life that the idea of being reborn appealed to her.

When she caught him staring she frowned. 'Do I have icicles running off my nose?'

Nic had no idea what possessed him, but he curled his arm about her waist, pulled her up against him and pressed his warm lips against her frozen little nose.

Just as before, she remained motionless. Not resisting, not exactly passive, but it was as if he held a vat of explosive energy that was too compressed and thought better of daring to move.

After a while he became concerned that she would pass out from lack of oxygen so he eased back. 'Better?'

A gorgeous flush pinkened her cheeks, but the pensive pleat in her brow said she didn't trust him as far as she could throw him. Which even he could admit wasn't very far.

Gingerly, she stepped backwards. 'Yes, thank you.'

'You're very welcome,' he said huskily, wanting her back in his arms, crushed tighter against him. 'So, are we the only guests here?'

'Afraid so. Other guests won't arrive for another week or two.'

She backed up another step, creating a gulf as vast and bleak as the Grand Canyon. If she wasn't the main player in his game of revenge he would be worried that the distance made him feel…empty.

'I think we should turn in for the night.'

'Let's not. The night is still young. I say we ditch our bags and hit the bar. Join me?' When she gave her head a little shake he unleashed the big guns and smiled with every ounce of sinful charm in his arsenal. 'Please, *bonita*?'

Hot loganberry juice warming her hands, Pia tipped her head back to gaze at a sky full of darkness and began to count the stars within a mind grid. When they didn't make an even number her clavicle started to itch so she started again. Anything to distract her from the man lounging obscenely close beside her—those dark bedroom eyes lingering on her throat as he threw out pheromones in great hulking waves.

There really shouldn't be anything sexy about a man padded out in warm gear, knocking back vodka as if it was mineral water.

Pia had coaxed him outdoors before he either drove her insane or destroyed the bar. His mere presence had cranked the temperature in the room so high she'd imagined the ice melting, pouring down the walls in silvery droplets until there was nothing left but the midnight stars.

Right then she felt the shift in the air. 'Wait for it… watch.'

'I am watching.'

'No, you're not, you're watching me.' And it was starting to annoy her. The contrived deceit of it. Why would Nic truly be interested in bedding a cold, uptight, neurotic mess like her? He wouldn't. This was a bet, a deal, and she'd do well not to go all jelly-legged next time he kissed her frozen nose. '*Now.* Look up.'

A whirlwind of pale green light appeared and swirled above, the streaks tossed about with abandon. Then dark red clouds of fire pulsated in waves and arcs, undulating against the midnight sky and darting towards the heavens.

It was a collision of energetic charged particles that never failed to make her heart float in her chest and her blood sing a chorus of joy that she was still alive.

'*Dios.* I take back everything I said. This is amazing, Pia. I've heard of the Northern Lights but this...'

'Aurora Borealis—named after Aurora, the Roman goddess of dawn, and Boreas, the Greek name for the north wind.'

Nic tutted good-naturedly. 'Should've known the Greeks would have something to do with it.'

Pia pursed her lips to contain a smile. Okay, so she had this fluttery feeling going on in her chest. It was bizarre. Not at all like the soft and gentle flapping of butterflies' wings people spoke of—no, no, no. More like pterodactyls swooping and clipping her heart with every pass. Actually, maybe bizarre was the wrong word. Terrifying was more like it.

She snuck a peek at him from the corner of her eye, then cursed herself for the urge.

Languid and sprawled out on the bench seat beside her, head tipped back, thick glossy hair curling in waves over his collar, he was simply too gorgeous for words. He was gazing upward, his whisky eyes full of awe and Pia shuddered with the need to taste the liquor glistening on his full mouth.

Why did looking at him make her want so much? Long for him to pull her into his arms.

The ache in her chest bloomed into self-disgust when he caught her staring and conjured up one of those glorious smiles that did odd things to her internal organs. Like jiggle them around a bit.

'What's the plan for tomorrow?' he asked.

'I'm touring some land where we're considering building more warm lodges. I'll be gone all morning.'

'*We* will be gone all morning,' he shot back, in that honed Carvalho dominating tone.

The very one she ignored.

'I can't see the huskies liking you, *Lobisomem*. They know a threat when they see it. Astute creatures.'

'I've never understood that moniker,' he said.

She didn't miss the way he'd brought the topic right back round to Zeus. She chalked up the ability to his incredibly shrewd mind. The *why* of it was what escaped her.

'Maybe Zeus saw a predator in you.'

'What's with the Greek mythological connotations anyway?'

'My great-grandfather started the club and he was obsessed with the stories. He was also a successful businessman in his own right, and if you ask me I'd say the control went to his head. In the years before he died he apparently believed himself a god. Sounds like a whacko to me.'

'Does your father believe himself a god, Pia?'

His voice was hard enough to shatter the bench they sat upon.

Had her father believed himself a god? 'I have no idea.' Sometimes she'd had no clue what had gone through his head.

'None? Are you saying you aren't close?'

She resisted the compulsion to shuffle in her seat. 'If you're speaking in terms of general proximity then no, we're rarely close.' She knew fine well he wasn't, but this was the last thing she wanted to discuss. Just prayed he'd drop it.

'I'm talking about emotions, *querida*, and you know it. A trip to the zoo when you were in pigtails. A loving face in the crowd at your school recitals. A celebratory meal when you passed your exams. Now sharing a bottle of wine and laughing over dinner, reminiscing over the good times. *Close.* As a father and daughter should be.'

A mass of stark yearning hit her shockingly hard in the solar plexus and she bowed forward, pretending to adjust the ties on her boots to ease the pain. She was unsure why she should feel that strongly, since her father had given her the important things in life—a roof over her head, food on the table and some measure of calm.

She sat upright and drank the last mouthful of loganberry, the sweet tartness exploding on her tongue. 'Not in the least,' she said. Only to wish the words back a second later. How pitiful they sounded. The empathy in his eyes didn't help. Whisky eyes, warm enough to melt her heart. *Impossible.*

'Any brothers or sisters?' he asked.

Translation: *Are you his only heir?*

Pia held an exasperated sigh in check. She wasn't sure how much longer she could take this. Every word, every touch had an ulterior motive. Most likely even his warmth and sincerity. And *still* there she was, cradling that soft, secret place inside her, hopelessly wishing he spoke the truth and wanted nothing more than to genuinely know her. Such a fool. She knew better.

'No brothers or sisters. You?'

'Only child too. One of those impossible dreams, but my mother… Well, let's say she wasn't particularly maternal.'

Join the club.

It wasn't until he said, 'Not close to her, then?' that she realised she'd said it out loud. Good God, she *had* to get away from him!

Digging her feet into the ground for a firm hold, she stood tall. 'I need some sleep. There's no need for you to come along tomorrow, so do yourself a favour and stay warm in your chalet bed.' *Give me some peace—leave me be, please.*

'You couldn't *pay* me to sleep on ice. I suppose to you it's like coffins for vampires.'

He said it with a wicked smile, as if he was trying to lighten the mood, but it went down like a lead balloon.

She gave him a withering glare. 'Aren't you hilarious? You should've been a comedian.' Though in a way he was right. She wanted the cold to numb the sensation of him, banish the heat he injected into her veins.

'I still don't understand what would possess you to sleep in the main hotel on packed ice. Believe me, if you knew what it was like to sleep on the streets—'

'It's an experience,' she said quietly, glancing at the doors to the Ice Castle with a painful kind of desperation.

'Ah,' he said derisively, and the change in him drew her eyes back to his. 'Like those celebrities who go to developing nations and starve just to know what it feels like. Except they can't *possibly* know what real, true, gripping hunger feels like. So if you're trying to prove something...'

On and on he went, and his tone got harder and more cynical. Right then he reminded her so much of her father that she started to shake and she...she... *Don't say it, Pia. Don't do it.*

Throat raw and swollen, every word hurt as they tore from her mouth. 'Maybe I do it not only for the experience but because I've been there, and I need to remember where I've come from so I can see what I've achieved. Maybe I like to feel the cold biting into my back in order to feel grateful that I'm one of the lucky ones and I now have a warm bed every night. And *that,* Mr Carvalho, is something I'll never take for granted. *Ever. Again.*'

Pia squeezed her eyes shut, hating both of them in that moment. She couldn't believe she'd just told him that.

Oh, come on, Pia, deep down you wanted him to know

*you've shared some of his darker days, that you have some-
thing in common. That you're more than the sum total of
your parts.*

Nic blinked up at her, jaw slack. 'When? I don't understand…'

'For the first seventeen years of my life. So don't you
dare judge me!'

'Where was your father?'

'I wouldn't know, okay? I didn't meet him until I was
seventeen. Now, if you'll excuse me, I need some sleep.'
Her voice sounded quivery and she hated it—*hated* it.
And—*oh, my God!*—the backs of her eyes were stinging.

'Hey, hey…' he said, launching from the bench and
reaching for her, strong arms wide open.

Pia backed away. 'Don't.' *Or I'll beg you to hold me and
I refuse to crumble, especially in front of you.*

He clenched his hands into fists and then raked his fingers through his hair. 'Okay, but let me come along in the
morning. I'd love to see the land. I promise no more talk of
your father—the past is out of bounds. I just want to spend
some time with you. Okay?'

She said nothing.

'Okay?' he repeated, this time adding a touch of concern and a dash of despair to his act. And that was the final
nail in *his* coffin.

CHAPTER SIX

SHE'D GONE WITHOUT him. The beautiful, obstinate, control freak that she was.

Nic let go of a sigh, heavy with annoyance and frustration.

One step forward, two steps back. For every tiny piece of information he squeezed from her she retreated farther away from him and he only had himself to blame. Pushing, pushing, *pushing* her to talk about her father, her past. Clearly that cool, calm composure had cracked under the strain.

The virtue of patience had been a blessing to him in the past few years. He'd had little choice but to bide his time. Until now. Now he wanted her surrender. *Needed* it to get to Zeus and destroy Q Virtus, he told himself for the millionth time. And yet…he *did* want to spend time with her.

The hell of it was, she intrigued him. He wanted to know how her mind ticked. How she juggled so many balls. What drove her. Why she hadn't known her father for the first seventeen years of her life.

So many questions that had nothing to do with taking Zeus to Hades and everything to do with the invisible rope that pulled him towards her when she was near. Like the *femme fatale* she was. Spell-binding him, luring him in, toying with him like a cat would a mouse.

His mouth twisted at the ridiculous notion. Nic knew

what he was doing, had a firm grip on the reins of his control, and no woman had the power to beguile him in deceit.

The log burner crackled, popped and hissed as he peered out of the window at the heavy grey skies, wondering how long she'd been gone and if she'd make it back in time before those laden clouds wept snow over the packed ice. An idyllic picture that struck him as nature's trick to disguise peril.

Nic smiled wryly and shook his head. Granted, he didn't feel like himself this morning, but now even the weather was duplicitous? What was more, the slosh and churn of worry inside him was a surprise he hadn't foreseen. Nor was the thought of her cosying up to her *friend* Jovan on a wooden slatted bench, covered in heavy fur rugs, being hauled by huskies across the snowy plains. A scene from some dreary romantic chick flick that likely flicked her switch. And why did that idea drive him to drink like a crazy *pessoa*?

Ah, careful, Nic. Jealousy will take you into the realms of obsession and beyond.

Like hell it would.

The irony of the situation knocked him sideways with the heft of a midfield striker. To anyone looking in there he was, waiting for the little wife to come home, and just like that he was staring at his father pacing the floors, fists clenched, waiting for Nic's mother to return from some shopping trip with friends, or lunch with her clique, or—worse—a night dancing about town. Always obsessing. Possessive. Angry when she wasn't home. Furious when she ignored him. Unstable. Erratic. Unnatural in Nic's eyes.

Narciso had asked him why he was considering marrying Eloisa Goldsmith. Truth was, while he'd loved his parents, after years of witnessing their volatile marriage he refused to sign up for the same fate.

Such love. Such passion. Such a hideous disaster.

His mood now a mire of filth, sucking him into the dangerous quicksand of the past, he slammed his feet into his boots and shoved his arms into the puffy warmth of his ski jacket. The thought of standing here waiting around for Olympia Merisi to grace him with her presence was taking him from vile to hostile.

Nic pulled the cabin door closed behind him and negotiated the packed ice, his feet crushing the thin dusting of new-fallen snow as he tramped down the path towards the main lodge. Huge white puffs of his breath formed in front of his face as he cursed the lack of Wi-Fi in his room. 'Going back to nature' translated to revisiting the Dark Ages as far as he was concerned.

The lodge greeted him with a warm blast of air and the sharp tang of espresso, but that, amazingly, wasn't the source of his overwhelming surge of relief. In the far corner of the main room sat Pia's sidekick, talking animatedly with another man, and he *hated* how the sight mollified him beyond measure. For pity's sake! He was not jealous. Or obsessed. He wasn't anything of the sort.

By the time he'd settled in front of his laptop and fired off a few e-mails to encourage the ruckus and fan the flames at Q Virtus he craved a long drink and his sanity. So he did what any sensible person would do in this situation. Rang his grandfather. To remind himself exactly why he'd chased a woman across Europe.

'Nicandro!' Instantly that gruff voice eased the tension that threatened to spiral out of control.

'Avô, how are you, old man?'

'Fine, fine, my boy. Just whooping Oscar here at Gin Rummy. Man doesn't know how to lose gracefully. Spat his teeth out twice in the last five minutes.'

Nic laughed out loud. 'You're a shark, Avô.'

'How was Zanzibar?'

'Hot.' In every way imaginable. Shocking. Satisfying. Frustrating. Nic condensed twenty-four hours of breaking and entering, gun-wielding, being tied to a chair and meeting the most stunning woman in the world to, 'Nothing to write home about.' Else the man would have heart failure and it was Nic's turn to look after *him*.

'Are you on your way back? I have a date with Lily tonight but I can put her on the back burner.'

Nic pictured that old Cary Grant style movie star face and silver hair. 'No, old man. No need. Go see Lily—enjoy yourself. I've stopped off in Finnmark, Norway. Minus fifteen if we're lucky.'

'*What?* Who the devil wants to go to Norway?'

Nic grinned, thinking they'd been almost his exact words.

'Forgot your origins, boy? Brazil—land of soccer and samba. A Santos needs heat. What's in Norway? A woman?'

Nic could hear the usual cacophony of chortles and chatter in the background and his heart ached. *Dios*, he missed this man. '*Sim*, Avô. A woman.'

'A special woman if Nicandro Carvalho traipses after her.'

Special? Yeah, she probably was. Not that it mattered.

'A necessary woman.' *If I'm to restore your glory. Place Santos Diamonds back in your hands before I lose you.*

The mere thought made Nic press his lips together and fight the sting at the back of his eyes. The fact that his grandfather had only a few good years left had kicked him into high gear, and he wouldn't downshift or stamp on the brakes until he'd reached the end of the road. A gift for the man who'd cradled him as a baby when his mother could not. Or maybe would not. What did it matter? Nic had still loved her like crazy. Her stunning face and her million-dollar sassy smile. She'd been zest and spirit and fiery heart and, yes, a big ol' handful of trouble—but there'd been something endearing about that. At least to him.

The one time she'd attended a football match she'd stood in seven-inch stilettos, a long cigarette in her hand, huge sunglasses covering half her face, yelling at the referee to 'Get that dirty brute off my son's back!' After that Nic had appealed to her well-deserved vanity, told her she distracted the players—no lie: her figure had stopped traffic—and asked her to stay away, else his reputation would have gone to the dogs.

His reflection in the window gazed back at him, wistful and nostalgic, and like a freight train another image rolled over him, just as vivid.

Himself at fourteen, when she'd picked him up from school—two hours late—raised a perfectly plucked brow and asked if he'd lost his virginity yet. He'd blushed and stammered and told her to shut up.

Hopeless in the maternal stakes, truly the farthest thing from a tree-hugging, celery-crunching supermom, but what she *had* been was a glorious, fun-loving woman who hadn't deserved to die. Certainly not with a cry lodged in her throat and a bullet in her head. Triggered by the man who—

Pain so acute it set his heart on fire made him gasp sharply, and he tried to cover the choking noise with a cough.

'Nic, my boy? What's wrong? Is there something you're not telling me?'

The concern in his grandfather's voice yanked him back to the here and now, just as it had done thirteen years ago and then continued for endless harrowing months as he'd harangued him to stand, then to walk—one small step, then two, then four. While Nic had bathed in a vile pit of despair and rage, wishing he'd just died in the same red river as his parents and the dreams of his youth.

There he'd been, dubbed the next Brazilian football sensation, destined to play with the best team in the world, lying with a bullet in his back. *Game over.*

Nic squeezed his eyes shut and cleared his throat. '*Non*, Avô. Everything is well. Everything is going to be just fine. As it should have always been.'

The sound of aged breathing, heavy from Cuban cigars and cognac told Nic he hadn't quite managed to disguise his turmoil.

'What have I always told you, Nicandro? Stand up, walk forward. Do not turn and look back or you will fall.'

Impossible. He was so at rock-bottom there was no void beneath him in which to plunge. *You also told me there were answers to be found, people to repay, legends to restore. So I stood and I walked forward to do just that.*

'Worry not, Avô. We'll talk again soon.'

'No, Nicandro, my boy, *wait*. Promise me you will return safe.'

'Always. *Tchau*, Avô.'

Nic's thumb pressed the 'end call' button and he gripped the handset as he stared beyond the glass. Beyond the cobwebs of frost glistening on the panes. Beyond the thick pelts of snow driving from the east. To the dark clouds laden with the promise of a continuous storm. Nature at its most dangerous.

By the time he'd sobered up he was frowning at the darkness. *Where are you,* querida*? Don't disappear on me now. I need you.* To quench this lust. To incinerate this incongruous need. To get him to Paris for the next step in his end game.

Sensing Jovan shift at his side, Nic shoved his fists inside his jacket pockets. 'She should've been back hours ago.'

Black eyes glared at him. 'Like you care. Or maybe you just care for the wrong reasons. I am on to you, Carvalho. You are not what you seem and I am watching you.'

The poor attempt to intimidate Nicandro Carvalho made him smile coldly. 'How does it feel to want a woman who doesn't want you back?'

'You tell me,' Jovan sneered, before walking away.

Nic's fists clenched with murderous intent as fire raged behind his ribs. Had she told her *friend* their chemistry was one-sided? Told him not to fret because she felt nothing but ice inside? Yet what really bothered him, he realised, was that the man might be right, and Nic felt his heart sink with the thought that she didn't desire him at all. That those seductively coy glances and the burning heat in her violet-blue eyes was all an act.

But what was seriously disturbing was that right now he couldn't care less. Either way, he wanted her back here. With him.

The striking solitary landscape was tinged with blue from the cold and deep orange from the sun's struggle towards the horizon and Pia breathed deeply, trying to ease the anxiety knotting her insides. Or was it guilt that she'd left without Nic?

'I'd love to see the land...spend time with you...'

He'd seemed so sincere, but every time she wanted to think the best of him she napalmed the idea.

'The storm is coming in, Miss Merisi. I vote we take a shortcut back to the Castle early. Either through the forest or across the lake.'

'One moment,' Pia told her guide, Danel, as she snapped another shot of the clearing. 'This land is perfect—especially with the salmon river close by for cold sea fishing.'

She'd taken enough photos. He knew it. She knew it. Problem was, she didn't want to go back. Not yet. She only wanted to ignore Nic's magnetic pull a while longer, to enjoy the beauty and tranquillity before he dragged her into another whirlwind of unwanted memories, unfathomable need and sleep deprivation.

'Miss Merisi, please. We must head back.'

Pia closed her eyes, inhaled a lungful of cleansing air and trudged back towards the sled. 'I don't mind which way—your call.'

'We'll cut across the lake. Much quicker.'

Once she'd settled in her seat the silence was broken by

the panting of the huskies and the soft whoosh of the sled gliding over crisp white snow. As they skirted the dense woodland of towering spruce the scent of pine infused her mind and the rhythmic rocking lulled her tired, sore eyes to close. As long as she didn't dream of her mother again—anything but that…

She must have dozed, because the next thing she knew the sled had jolted sharply to the left and the sound of spooked huskies filled her ears with piercing whimpers.

Pia bolted upright. 'What's wrong?' Then she shivered violently as streaks of icy water ran down her face, soaked her hair. God, she must have been out of it.

Danel struggled with the reins as snow thrashed against his face. 'Storm came out of nowhere. Hold on—we'll take cover in the forest.'

Fear lodged in her chest and she gripped the edge of the bench until her knuckles screamed. *Don't panic. You've been through worse, far worse than this.*

The sled veered right, the movement holding her on a knife-edge. Visibility was virtually non-existent, and then it all happened so fast her head spun.

The sled tipped. The sound of grinding wood tore through her ears. As did the distinct crack of ice.

Danel yelled over the furious howl of the wind, his words muffled. Obscured. Then she was tossed up into the air like a ragdoll, only to plunge to the hard-packed surface, the agonising crash sending pain shooting through her body.

A cry ripped from her throat, then her head smacked off the unforgiving lake and her last thought—that she'd done the right thing, was glad she'd left without Nic and he was safe back in his cabin—was obliterated as the lights went out.

He'd had enough. Nic couldn't take it any more.

The thundering, purposeful stride that had brought him

to this place, this woman, took him to the manager's suite on the other side of the lodge via the snow that swirled in eddies and whorls, whipping at his skin and biting through his clothes.

Nic burst through the door, sending papers flying off the desk. 'I want a search party out there for the last hour of light. She's been gone too long.'

'We don't have anyone to send—'

'I'll go myself. Give me a map of their route and get me a four-by-four. I can ice-drive with the best of them.'

'I am sure all is well, sir. I—'

'Do it. *Now.*' His lethal voice caromed around the room and he watched the ruddy complexion of the man pale and bead with sweat. And all the while Nic's guts roiled with worry and dread and an outcome that didn't bear thinking about.

Nor did the reasons why.

CHAPTER SEVEN

PIA'S TEMPLES THROBBED, pain swirled around her head, but worst of all she was cold. So cold. And she was so tired of being cold.

This couldn't be real, but it felt so much like reality it was frightening. She kept having brief flickers of *déjà-vu* as hands grabbed her arm, manacling her at the shoulder and wrist, bruising as they pinned it to the bed.

'No, no, *please*—get off me!'

White light flickered in front of her closed eyelids, the black beats in between like snapshots of time replaying in her mind…

Voices. Her mother's shrill. And Pia knew Mama was on the ledge again, fighting with an opium haze of madness, because her panic slithered through the cracks in Pia's basement door like curling wisps of smoke, threatening to choke her.

Karl yelled, 'We've gotta run—they're coming after us.'

Pia's legs buckled as drawers opened and slammed shut. Drug money. The dealers. Coming after them. *Oh, God.*

'It's her damn fault, that useless kid of yours. No good for nothing. She didn't take the money.'

No, no! When she'd gone to deliver the money they'd wanted far more than cash from her and she'd run. *It wasn't her fault—it wasn't. It really wasn't.*

'So we'll take her to Merisi and he can pay seventeen years of child support so we can disappear.'

Pia froze, ear pressed against the hollow door as the bottom fell out of her world. Child support? She had a daddy?

'To Zeus? No, Karl, he'll kill me.'

Her mother's voice shook. She was terrified.

'He doesn't know.'

Kill her? He sounded worse than *this* nightmare. She'd be trading one hell for another.

Nails black, deeply encrusted with dirt, Pia clawed at the door. Heart thumping frantically. *Don't leave me here, Mama. Take me with you. Please. I'll be better. I'll be good—do whatever you want. Just please take me with you.*

Then they were in Pia's room and holding her down, and she was thrashing and twisting and trying to sink her teeth into the arm that was pinning her hard.

'No, no, *no*—get off me!'

A big hand slapped across her cheek, setting her skin on fire, but she just got back up and clawed and hissed and screamed for her life.

Until that cold metal pricked her arm and freezing liquid seeped into her veins and peace finally stole her pain.

Memories, always ready with daggers—as Nic knew—were stabbing her subconscious, making her voice a wavering chord of desperation as she lay half-naked and ghastly pale beneath a blanket on his bed.

He couldn't keep still—just paced back and forth alongside while her slow, shallow breathing and mumbles and cries gripped him by the throat. He should have searched for her sooner. Another hour lying on the cracked ice of the lake, soaked through to the skin, and she would have been dead. Another hour from now and she *would* die if they couldn't warm her up. Hypothermia had set in, and unless she calmed down and allowed the drips...

Dios, she looked so vulnerable. *Was* so vulnerable. It was a fist in his heart as he remembered what it felt like to feel paralysed.

Another shriek ricocheted off his taut nerves.

'Do something, for heaven's sake!'

The man who *claimed* to be the senior of the two medics hovering tried to hold her arm still once more, but her every contorted muscle and frozen vein screamed genuine fear.

Pia brushed down her arms, her movements frantic yet uncoordinated as she shivered and slurred. 'Please...*please*, no! Don't do this.'

On and on she went, crying out for her mama, then talking of Merisi, Zeus—private, personal nightmares—and he *hated* it. Hated that she was baring her soul in such an anguished, agonising way in front of complete strangers. He wanted them gone. Would have banished them from the room if he could.

Instead he said, in a voice that brooked no argument and warned of dire consequences, 'She's delirious—has no idea what she's saying or doing.'

Nic watched silvery tears trickle down her temples as her energy depleted and she turned to look him right in the eye. '*Please*...don't...do this to me.'

That was it. That heart-wrenching plea coming from a woman like Pia was the final straw.

'Stop. Just *stop*! Her heart must already be at risk from the strain, and if she gets any more worked up—'

'She needs to get warm quickly. Intravenous fluids are the way to go. Unless we bypass her blood, warm it through, but that's still going through a vein.'

'That's it? Those are our options? *Dios!*' His voice sounded as if he'd swallowed a razorblade. He couldn't stand seeing her like this. It made him want to crawl out of his own skin.

'My only other suggestion would be for you to get in there. Skin to skin. It'll probably take longer, but it should still work.'

Right—*right*. Why hadn't he thought of that? *Because she obliterates your brain cells, that's why.*

'This would have been useful ten minutes ago,' he gritted out. With a deft roll of his shoulders his heavy coat slipped down his back and he tossed it over the nearest chair.

'We didn't think there would be a problem, and...' This from the second medic. A tall redhead who was staring at his hands as he uncuffed his shirt.

'You may leave.' He punctuated the words by grabbing his shirt at the tails and tearing it open.

The redhead's lips parted and colour flushed her white skin as buttons bounced off walls and pinged off the floors. He toed off his shoes and went to work on his trousers and her eyes trailed down his flexing biceps, across his wide chest, then paused as he hooked his thumbs into the waistband of his briefs.

Fighting the shivers that could only have come from being outside half the night in minus fifteen freaking degrees, Nic stared down at Pia, lying on the bed, eyes closed, trembling.

Commando or not?

She was out of it, but he didn't want her waking up in his bare arms being frightened. Didn't want her to think he'd taken advantage of her for a second. *Innocent* wasn't a word he would associate with her, but where sex was concerned, or being comfortable naked, in your own skin...? He wasn't so sure about that.

'I can leave her bra and panties on, yes?'

'They look insubstantial enough, so I doubt they'd make much difference.'

'From this moment it is not your place to look,' he growled, throwing in a lethal glare for good measure. Ridiculous as it was, his protective instincts had kicked in with a ferociousness that astounded him. 'I repeat. You may leave.'

He ushered them out through the door, agitated by the way the redhead was devouring him with her eyes. Why couldn't Pia look at him like that? Then maybe she wouldn't have swanned off without him this morning and he would have been there all along to keep her safe.

Once he'd locked his door behind them he was back to the bed, fingers flexing on the corner of the blanket. Nervous? Eager? He didn't know. His concern was so overwhelming it drowned every other emotion out.

Gingerly, he pulled the covers back, just enough to allow him to slip beneath. Nic tried to shut off every thought in his head, loath to admit to the arousing anticipation of feeling those lush curves against him. Then he sent up a prayer of thanks that he'd kept her in her underwear as— *Fala serio*, could someone cut him some slack, *please*?— frivolously skimpy as it was.

Under the covers, he didn't pause to take a breath, not wasting a second of time when his heat could be seeping into her body, protecting her life.

It hit him then. What he was doing. Saving the daughter of the man who'd destroyed his parents and almost taken Nic's life. He could hurt Zeus in the same way—make him feel the same pain Nic had felt for so long. An eye for an eye. But the fact was it wasn't in him. Not even if Pia had pulled the trigger herself. He simply wasn't made that way. Life was too precious to take.

No pause, no hesitation, he tucked one arm under her shoulders and eased her against him, front to front, skin to skin, cheek to cheek. All her softness against his hard strength. Cold flesh against heat. He'd expected a struggle, at least a murmur of protest. What he got was a contented purr when, like a kitten, she burrowed and nuzzled closer, as if trying to climb into his body, where it was warm, so she could go to sleep, protected and safe.

Nic cupped her head, tucked her into the warm space where his neck met his shoulder and gently wrapped his leg around hers until they were one, until the only thing that could be missing was his hardness sliding inside her.

Oddly enough, this felt closer—an affection he'd never experienced before. Far more intimate than sex could ever be.

Nic lay there, holding her, gently stroking her hair, burying his nose in the damp waves, inhaling the cold scent that lingered on her body and there…right *there*…was the faintest hint of that velvety black scent she wore like a sultry signature: jasmine and gardenia and something elusive that sang to his body in a siren's song. And, *Dios*, it turned him to stone. He shifted and cursed under his breath, trying his damnedest to ignore the lush satiny dips and curves that fitted perfectly against him.

Tried, too, to quieten every alarm bell shrilling in his head, not to think about what might have been for the first seventeen years of her life. *Too late.*

At the age when Nic was kicking a football around a field and fishing in the river with his Avô, with not a concern or care in the world for anyone or anything, Pia had been living in her own kind of hell. The fact that she'd been subjected to drugs and abuse from her own mother made him want to lash and snarl and bite like the werewolf she claimed him to be. He realised, too, that her father must have taken her in, taken care of her…

It was a conflicting choking agony to want to feel gratitude to the man who'd caused his parents' deaths, if only for a second. It tore at his heart even to think it. Yet he was glad Pia had found a better life and a reason for living.

'Is that why you work so hard for him?' he whispered as he kissed her flaxen hair.

Nic finally allowed himself to think of the high likelihood that he'd take Pia down with her father. It made his ribcage contract but he'd come too far for too long to be swayed by emotions now. *She'll hate you. Yes, she will.*

He flinched as she startled him with a soft reply.

'Keep me,' she breathed.

What was she saying? That she worked so hard so her father would keep her?

Nic squeezed his eyes shut and used every weapon at his disposal, every memory he could find, to banish the tumultuous thoughts storming through his mind.

She whimpered and Nic hushed her. 'Sleep *querida*, I have you.' For now.

CHAPTER EIGHT

PIA TRIED TO rouse herself time and again from the murky waters of sleep but it kept tugging her back into the nebulous depths. First there'd been darkness and moonlight, then the glare of the midday sun, but her bones had ached so badly she'd snuggled back into the hard-packed mattress and let it happen.

Not this time. Now the warm scent of expensive cologne tempted and teased her senses awake. Skin and a light dusting of soft hair against her cheek—warm, so warm, and achingly wonderful. She sighed in contentment.

She felt as if she'd slept for days, and as she coaxed her eyes open to the golden fingers of dusk stroking the windowpane she wondered if that were true.

Had she ever been so lazy and sweet inside? Never—

Pia jerked upright so fast the room spun like a whirly top. What the—?

Her gaze snapped to Nic, lying beside her, and her belly clenched with hot longing at the sight of him—so strong, so masculine, and yet so vulnerable. Face relaxed, as if sleep was his only peace, those long sooty black lashes rested against the tender skin beneath his eyes in decadent arcs.

She was dying to run her hand over his defined chest, that rigid six-pack and his flat, ripped stomach, the hipbones jutting just shy of his boxers…

Then it hit her. He was practically naked. And so was she!

'*Nic…?*' Grabbing the sheet, she covered her breasts and

bottom-shuffled sideways to the edge of the bed. What had he done to her? What had *they* done? 'You…you…snake!'

Stretching with all the lethargic might of a big sleepy lion basking in the sun, he blinked up at her over and over, as if clearing the fog from his eyes. It took a while, and Pia just sat there watching him, her mind all over the place, trying to figure out how on earth she'd got into his bed. Then suddenly he snapped wide awake, and looked so ridiculously happy to see her that her heart leapt.

'You're awake?'

Pia pinched the back of her hand in self-test mode. 'I'd like to say that's a stupid question, but actually I have no idea.' Maybe she was still asleep and this was a dream. *A dream, Pia? Don't you mean a nightmare?*

He grinned wildly. 'Yep, there's that sharp tongue I like so much. You are definitely awake, *bonita*. You had me worried for a while there.'

When his hot gaze dropped to her lace bra he stared at her so hard she craved a shower. Whether hot or cold she couldn't say. Why did every day with him feel like Russian Roulette?

'Don't think for one minute this constitutes the terms of our bet!' At least she hoped to God it didn't. It rather depended on what had happened. Why couldn't she remember? This was awful. *Awful!*

Mischief sparkled in his whisky eyes, lighting them up with flecks of gold as he rolled onto his side playfully and propped his head on one hand. 'I didn't take you for a shirker, *querida*. You *did* beg.'

'I…I…I did?' She had? *Noooo.*

Nic raised one devilish brow and ran his tongue over that gorgeous mouth suggestively. 'Oh, yeah. I told you no over and over again, but would you listen?' He shook his head and tutted. 'No.'

There he was, the perfect picture of dissolute debauchery, tiptoeing his fingers over the rumpled linen and giving her thigh a sultry little stroke.

Pia shuddered and grappled with the blanket to cover her legs, but he was sprawled over them and he couldn't give a stuff—just smiled that bone-melting, tummy-flipping smile and kept on talking.

"'I'm cold, Nicandro.'"

The way he imitated her voice in a brazen purr and batted his eyelashes made her recoil in horror.

"'Please come to bed with me. I neeeeed you. Please.'"

She gasped in outrage at her own behaviour. Mentally scanned her body parts for sensations of wear and tear. Wear and tear? What was she? *A car?*

Okay, so she couldn't remember what *après sex* felt like, but she was darn sure she would feel something—right?

During her moments of castigation, as her mind flitted like a bird from one branch to another, he'd tugged the blanket away and inched closer, prowling like a feral wolf with hunger in his eyes. Pia looked down and watched his long fingers splay over the slight curve of her stomach, then curl around her waist.

Heat sizzled over her skin and her breath grew so shallow she began to hyperventilate.

'Come here, my beautiful Olympia. Kiss me. Just as you did last night.'

A tight, choking disbelief caught her by the throat. But there was no calculation in his eyes, none of the shrewdness she'd noticed in him before, and this joyful, impish innocence was a sharp deviation when she knew he had the tail of a scorpion.

Worse still, when had she got so lonely that she didn't care? Just wanted him near her.

'What did you do to me?' she asked, voice trembling as her pulse careened out of control.

Oh, God, she felt angry, and helpless, and frustrated that

she couldn't remember. But most of all—most alarmingly of all—she felt cheated!

With that thought, she tumbled backwards off the bed and landed in a sprawled heap. No grace to it whatsoever. Then she scrambled to her feet and edged away.

Predator. That was surely the word to describe him in that moment as he crawled across the mattress on all fours—big and agile and poetry in motion—the wickedness in his eyes making her lick her dry lips.

'Ah, you want me to *chase* you?' He drew the word out and added a naughty lilt to it.

'No!'

He sighed theatrically, as if they'd been through all this before. 'Which means yes.'

'No, it really doesn't! What is *wrong* with you?' He was being so frisky and light-hearted. Worlds apart from the practised charmer she'd come to expect.

And his body... *Wow.* All sex and power. The man might be Brazilian but he was like a Greek god. Broad shoulders and carved pecs, rounded thighs and long, athletic sculpted legs sprinkled with dark hair. Quite simply, he was delicious.

Slam. Her back hit the wall and he pressed up against her and thrust his hands into her hair. 'Shall I remind you, Pia? Remind you of the taste of my mouth?'

Yes. *Yes!* Nooooo—bad idea. Really.

She remained frozen, her blood pumping too fast in some places and too slowly in others. Her brain, for instance—no blood at all in there.

Nic cupped the back of her head, his fingers the perfect amount of tingly pressure on her scalp, and leaned in. He kissed the rim of her ear, nibbled on her lobe and whispered, 'Try to remember this one, would you, *bonita*?'

'I don't think...we've done this before.' Because it felt as if she was on the edge of discovery, at the gates of a bold new world. And it was exhilarating and scary all at once.

Electricity arced between them, the shock so violent that Nic jerked back an inch or two and locked onto her eyes. As they stared at one another, her breasts brushed against the hard wall of his chest with every stuttering breath she took. Heaven help her, she wanted it. *Him.* His kiss. Right now.

'You make me crazy, Pia,' he murmured, his gaze intense and considered. His breath a hot rush over her face. 'You turn me inside out and that is the honest truth.'

Leaning in, he touched his lips to hers and she felt as if she'd been plugged into the national power grid. Closing her eyes, she started to panic. Unsure if she could remember how to respond.

Then he laved his tongue along her lips and she opened up, unfurling to him, giving him her all. And in that moment she didn't think or plan or have an agenda. She simply moved and gave him permission to go deep and wet and erotic. Which was exactly what he did, with a feral growl that made her skin tighten.

One hand on her lower back, another between her shoulderblades; he pressed her sweetly but firmly against him. She'd never felt anything like it. Unbearably wonderful.

Pia squirmed closer. He pulled her tighter. *More.* More of the languorous touch of his tongue against her own. And she moaned at the sharp, masculine taste of him—potent and alluring.

It was the hottest, raunchiest, most sensual kiss she'd ever received in her life. He was practically licking her soul.

Nic tightened his hold and she went pliant, revelling in this place where neither of them was alone, letting her body bend to his will as the terror of yearning and the thrill of feeling overwhelmed her.

He started talking out a scene—what he craved doing to her—the words rolling lyrically from his talented mouth.

'I want to taste you everywhere, learn every dip and curve of your beautiful body, feel every inch of you in my hands.' He punctuated the words with the movement of those clever fingers, trailing down her arms—leaving goosebumps in his wake—then sliding them up her ribcage to cup her lace-covered breasts. Just that slight ease of pressure off her shoulders, the heat emanating from his touch, was the most delicious sensation on earth.

He kissed words along her jaw and ground his hips, pushing his groin against her. Pia moaned long and loud as the hot flesh between her legs beat a wanton tattoo and clenched, desperate for him to be inside her.

'I want to feel your surrender, Pia. Will you give it to me?'

Another kiss. Another hard press. More heat curling through her veins, swirling through her abdomen.

'I want to slide down your body and take your orgasm in my mouth. I would do anything…*anything* to taste you. Just once. Before I thrust into your glorious body and take you to heaven and back.'

She squirmed, gyrating back against him.

'You'd love that, wouldn't you, Pia? Me inside you. Taking you long and hard and deep.'

Yes. *Yes*.

Next thing Pia knew, she had *his* back plastered against the wall and she was kissing *him* ferociously—her hands in his thick glossy hair, up on her toes so his huge thick erection nudged her lace panties—unleashing a torrent of carnal need she'd had no idea she was capable of. The scent of him, the feel of his hard body under her seeking hands, was so heady she couldn't get enough. It sent her hormones, her adrenaline, her desire for him into orbit. And when he fisted her hair with one hand and squeezed her left breast with the other stars burst behind her eyelids.

Nic groaned. She almost climaxed. And the shock of it, of being so out of control, burning from the inside out, was like an arrow of ice spearing into her psyche.

Ice.

Mortification prickled over her skin and she wrenched away from him.

'You are ice and fire, Pia,' he breathed, that wide chest heaving.

Ice. *Ice.* Huskies whimpering. Ice cracking. Freezing water seeping into her skin.

'You…you…' It was worrying that that was all the eloquence she had. But, honestly, she was turning into a vacuous bimbo without a lick of sense. He was playing with her!

'Are a good kisser?' he suggested, still breathless, still too suave and sinful for his own good. '*Sim*, I know. You aren't too bad yourself. Come back here and we'll practise some more.'

The way he was looking at her was scary. As if he had voodoo powers—whether for evil or for good she *still* didn't know. But it was the kind that made her think he would keep her drugged on sex for weeks if she let him.

Never in a month of Sundays!

'You, *Lobisomem,* are the lowest of the low.'

Face flushed, he cocked an arrogant brow. 'You weren't saying that when you had your tongue down my throat, *querida.*'

'That was before I remembered the snowstorm. When was that? Yesterday? What happened? How did I get back here?'

He raked a palm across the high ridges of his abdomen as if his chest ached. 'I found you.'

Nic had come looking for her? 'Did you find Danel, too?'

'Yes. He fared a little better than you and came to visit earlier. And, before you ask, the huskies are also fine. They ran for cover in the forest.'

'Good. That's…good.' It hurt even to think, and when she tentatively rubbed the sore mound on the side of her head she winced at the deep throb of pain.

Okay. So he'd rescued them. But—

'How did I end up in your bed?' And on the verge on surrendering! 'Clearly you would've slept with me, taken advantage, just to win a bet,' she said scathingly. 'You would've let me believe it was too late!'

A dimple popped in his cheek as he clenched his jaw and those eyes grew dark with shadows. 'No. Instead I would've stopped before we'd gone too far. Told you you'd been sick with hypothermia and frightened of the needles, and that if I hadn't climbed into bed with you to warm you up death would've been mere hours away.'

Pia swayed where she stood, clinging to hostile suspicion as if it were a life raft. A raft that bobbed and tipped precariously as she recalled waking time and again, wrapped in a cashmere mist: Nic holding her tight, as if she were something precious.

He'd saved her life. First by searching for her and then holding her throughout the night and well into the day. Never moving from her side. And his touch hadn't been grudging or just necessary, because he wanted something in return. It had felt cherishing, gentle, almost covetous. A touch she'd never felt before but wanted to again. Desperately.

Tears stung the backs of her eyes. Not because she was hurting or upset or distressed but because the torrent of strange contrary sensations was close to overload. She was fighting this thing between them with everything she had, and right now it was breaking her.

It had to be the close call with death making her so emotional. *Had* to be.

Nic's sudden launch off the wall made her flinch, and she panicked in case she'd been staring with no filter on.

'I did what I had to do,' he said, brisk and decisive.

Pia could literally see him gathering up the tattered remnants of his control.

'Had to?' she repeated stupidly, commanding her body to stand tall, chin up, projecting nonchalance.

Bending at the waist, he swiped a T-shirt from the floor. One that looked as if it had been tossed away haphazardly in haste.

Smoothing the crumpled material down his chest, he finally met her eyes—and the sardonic smile he tipped her way wasn't quite right. It was sort of forced into hardness, and it made her stomach dive to the rug.

'Oh, I get it,' she said, imposing upon her tone its usual sass. 'How can you win our bet if I'm six feet under, right?'

He didn't bother denying it, just shoved his limbs into clothes as if he wanted nothing more than to run from the room.

All the happiness and wonder and joy from that life-shattering kiss drained out of her and in the void—as if clearing the toxic mess of emotions had given her the space to think clearly again—she picked over his words.

'Frightened? I was frightened of the needles?' Good God, what had she said?

'Petrified, Pia.'

He was looking at her so oddly she couldn't catch her breath. A humourless laugh was trapped in her throat, fluttering, as if she'd swallowed a moth. A choking, frantic tickle.

'Did I talk much? Say anything…interesting?'

A surge of shame hit her with the stunning force of a tidal wave as her filthy past crashed over her, coating her in anguish and dread. The possibility that Nicandro Carvalho might know where she'd come from, who she'd been. The damage he could cause her with that kind of information at his disposal. *But he doesn't know that you're Zeus. Just keep it together.*

'You made little sense, Pia, and said nothing of interest to anyone, I assure you.' All this talking was while he avoided her gaze, and she was positive he wasn't telling her the entire story.

Was he saying her secrets were safe with him? Could she

trust that? Maybe she could, because otherwise he would have pushed for more, just as he always did. Poked and prodded until he uncovered a rotting bed of grime.

'Pia!'

It wasn't until Nic shouted her name from across the room that she realised she was about to keel over.

'*Dios!* I'm such an idiot. You shouldn't even be out of bed. You'll be weak for days.'

'Your concern is so touching,' she jeered, covering her embarrassment with sweet sarcasm.

He swept her up into his arms as if she weighed no more than a child and walked across the floor, his bare soles slapping on the hardwood, before gently lowering her to the bed.

Pulling the blankets over her, he tucked her in. She shouldn't adore the extraordinary contentment of being fussed over, and nor should she consider going to the bathroom so he'd do it all over again.

'You are still sick, Pia. No more cold. No more ice. Tonight you sleep in my bed and tomorrow morning, when the sun rises, I'm taking you somewhere warm.'

Not a chance. 'If I'm sleeping in this bed, *you* are on the couch—and what's more I'm not going anywhere *warm*. I have a stay-over in Munich and then—'

'I don't care if you have a meeting with the Queen of England at Buckingham Palace. We made a deal. I came here—now it's your turn to go where I wish. I have business in Barcelona, so to Barcelona we shall go.'

She didn't like that look. That arrogance and audacity and command. It was a powerful combination of traits that had made him a dominant force in real estate and one of the most sought-after men in the world.

'And if I say no?'

'You'll be breaking the terms of our deal and I'll take that as forfeit,' he said, with lethal softness.

'What terms?' She pulled the sheets higher over her

body, practically up to her nose. A bit late, of course, but her pride was on the floor in tatters and she needed all the help she could get.

'To spend time with me.'

Pia filled in what he wasn't saying. *To prove I am not so bad. To let me gain your trust.*

Yeah, right.

Collapsing back onto the pillows, she closed her eyes. He had a point. Fact was, she had little choice but to follow him. She still needed answers, needed to know if Nic was behind the propaganda, and she'd given her word. So she'd just have to play nice with the other children and compromise.

'Fair's fair, I suppose. I'll have to cancel my meeting in Munich.' She'd swear she could feel hives pop from her skin. Skin that begged for the scrape of her nails.

'You say that as if it's the end of the world. You've never cancelled a meeting before? Ever?'

'No.'

He paused with his arm halfway into the sleeve of his jacket and looked up. His hair was a tousled mess from her fingers. So gorgeous. 'Do you ever stop? Even for a moment?'

No. 'Why would I?'

'To live. Have fun. See friends. Be happy.'

'I do live.' She had no idea what fun was. As for friends—she didn't have the time. 'I am happy.' *Liar.* Pia and happiness were barely on speaking terms. And since when was she bothered?

She wished she could hit him right now.

'You keep telling yourself that while I head over to the lodge. I need to make the travel arrangements to Spain.'

Barcelona.

It was a horrible mistake. It had all the hallmarks of a

tragic ending. In fact she was starting to feel like the lead in a Shakespearean comedy.

So why was she sitting here, handing over control, waiting for him to turn the next page?

CHAPTER NINE

NIC SLAMMED THE Bugatti into fifth gear, pushed his foot to the floor and spun down the B-10 coast road heading into the heart of Barcelona town. On his right, the long sun-drenched waterfront skimmed the blue crystalline waters of the Balearic and on his left reclining in her seat, was the woman who was turning him inside out.

With a need for speed that echoed the years that had passed he drove himself harder, farther, faster. Running from his mournful memories or towards his predestined future, he wasn't sure.

This was all getting a bit close to home, he thought wryly, his accusation to Pia still fresh in his mind. *'Do you ever stop? Live. See friends. Be happy.'*

The hypocrisy of his words didn't escape him. Avô was rather fond of telling him he needed to slow down, play harder, be happier.

Happy? He couldn't remember the last time he'd felt the sweet tendrils of joy curl around his heart and lift the cumbersome weight of rage. Before yesterday, that was. His relief at seeing Pia up and about had floored him and he didn't want to over-analyse that. It certainly didn't mean he was developing any sort of...*feelings* for her. That would take the crowning glory for stupid moves on his part.

But, if he was being totally honest with himself, for the first time in years his purposeful stride had faltered. Nic would never forget the look on Pia's face—the fear that he knew of her past, the shame that had eviscerated the beautiful pink flush after his kisses.

Yes, okay, he'd wanted to push—to ask why, to dig, to find something he could use to demolish her father. Instead he'd stood there and looked into those exquisite violet-blue eyes, with the sultry taste of her lingering in his mouth and hadn't been able to do it. Couldn't make her relive it. Only wanted to soothe her, help her forget, make it all disappear. Not cause more pain while he was rocking her world, shaking the foundations she'd built her pride upon.

She'd never forgive him, but there was little likelihood they'd meet again after his meeting with her father. Nic would go back to New York and likely marry Goldsmith's daughter, place Santos Diamonds back in Avô's hand. As for Pia, she was strong. The strongest woman he'd ever met. She would close this chapter in her life, stand up and move on, doubtless ruing the day they'd met.

Hands white on the steering wheel, he breathed through the tightness in his chest.

It wasn't as if Pia would be left with nothing, he assured himself. Merisi seemed like an octopus, with tentacles that reached far and wide, so Nic doubted he'd ever know the full extent of his business interests. But one thing he would never falter on—Q Virtus must fall. The coliseum that had held the gladiatorial battle of Santos versus Merisi and witnessed his family's demise. And Zeus must be exposed for the crook he was.

Then he could crawl beneath a rock, as far as Nic cared. Maybe he'd leave Pia to manage what Nic had left alone. He hoped so, because he didn't want Pia starting again from nothing. Not after what she'd been through.

Nic was more anxious than ever to meet the man. Q Virtus was finally cracking under his strain, and by the time they reached Paris the vast majority of members would have disowned it, never to return. Nic had given them enough doubt to disease their minds and ensure they jumped ship while their reputations and businesses were still intact. He couldn't wait to see the look in the other man's eyes when faced with his nemesis. Couldn't wait to tell him his club and the Merisi legacy were dying.

Dammit, he *needed* that meeting. He just had to bed Pia to get there.

The thought was a mighty hand at his throat that gripped without remorse. Why was he suddenly uncomfortable with the idea? It wasn't as if he was seducing her under duress—she wanted him just as much as he wanted her. Mutual pleasure was theirs for the taking, and if the attraction between them had been strong before, now it was off the charts. As if they'd tasted nirvana and craved another shot.

Barcelona town came into view—all grandiose architecture and Gothic flair—and he sneaked a sideways glance at his temptress.

With the top down in his ferocious little supercar, the wind had whipped at that perfect film noir up-do as if taunting her to cut loose and gave her cheeks a healthy lustrous glow of pink. The hypothermia had taken its toll, and she'd slept for most of the flight, but out in the warm air, with huge sunglasses covering half her face, a small smile teasing her mouth, head tipped back as she looked up at the children waving from the bridge, he thought she'd never looked more beautiful. Or so young.

'You know…take away the laptop and the phones and the bodyguards and you look twenty years old, *querida*.'

Pia rolled her head on the cushioned pad to face him and her eyebrows shot skyward. 'How old do I look *with* them?'

'All serious and scowling? Forty at least.' Hideous exaggeration, but he was all for inflation to make his point and get a rise.

'Oh, charming! I thought you were aiming for my bed—not to get pushed off the roof!'

Nic threw his head back and laughed. He couldn't remember the last time a woman had made him laugh, made him lie in wait for the next outrageous thing to come out of her mouth, made him want to find the nearest bed and touch that sinuous, sultry body again. Ice and fire personified.

'So, unless you want me to think the worst you'll have to tell me how old you are.'

'Didn't anyone ever tell you never to ask a woman her age?'

Blame it on the sunshine. Blame it on the town he'd always loved and the opportunity to show it to Pia since she'd confessed she was a virgin to these parts and he suspected her travels were devised for oppressive boardroom play. Hell, blame it on the laughter in his heart, but the words just tumbled out.

'*Sim*, my mother. She used to pay me to tell my friends she was ten years younger. Said she would rather carry the stigma of teenage pregnancy than be seen as old. Mamãe was a great lamenter that you're only as young as you feel.'

Sabrina Santos would have liked Pia, he decided—very much. Talk about irony.

'You speak of her in the past tense. Did you lose her?'

Nic could feel her scrutiny burning into his cheek and found swallowing past the emotional grenade in his throat was harder than he'd expected. 'Yes. A long time ago. Both of my parents are dead.'

Gripping the gearstick, he downshifted as pedestrian traffic became dense and he could see children lining the streets. Distracted as he was, when he felt the startling yet unbearably sweet stroke of the back of Pia's finger down his ear and jaw he flinched.

'I'm sorry, Nic. Your mother sounds like she was a hoot. You must miss her. Miss them both.'

More than you could ever know—and I have your father to thank for it.

The violent need for vengeance flared back to life and it took everything he had to keep his emotions in check. The air grew taut with an uncomfortable silence and from nowhere he wished she would touch him again, so he could feed off a comfort he really didn't deserve.

Instead she filled the quiet. 'Well, if she was right, some days I feel one hundred.'

'But not today.'

'No,' she said softly. 'Not today. This place is just…so stunning. Amazing.'

She raised her arms in the air and he imagined she could feel the cool breeze kiss her palms, whistle through her fingers.

'If I tell you how old I am, will you answer me a question honestly?'

'I'll try my very best,' he hedged.

'I'm twenty-eight.'

Dios, very young. He hadn't expected that. It wasn't that she looked older; it was the way she carried the weight of the world on her shoulders almost effortlessly at times. Then again, with her past, he imagined she'd had to grow up quickly—much as he had.

'So…' she began, threading her fingers into a prayer-hold, knuckles white.

Her pregnant pause made his stomach pitch.

'Have you ever had any business dealings with Antonio Merisi, my father?'

Personally? 'No.'

'I'll never have sex with you, Nic.'

He didn't miss the hard core of determination or the frayed edges of remorse. She desired him, but with this damn bet between them… He was beginning to see the error of his arrogant ways there. One look and all he'd been able to think of was taking her, having her body beneath him, cocksure she'd tumble into his arms within hours. The woman screamed *sex* and he hadn't seen past that *femme fatale* persona. But beneath the façade was a vulnerability that made him ache.

'Why don't you just tell me why you want to meet him,

tell me what the problem is, and I'll try and fix it. I'll find a way. It's the least I can do after you…'

'Saved your life, Pia? Held you in my arms for hours on end?'

Nic waited until he'd pulled to a stop at a crossing before glancing over at her—she was staring at the Barcelonians cluttering the pavement, the back of her hand pressed against her mouth. He'd give his eye teeth to know what she was thinking.

'You can't help or fix it,' he said, wishing she could with all his heart. 'I don't want to discuss him, Pia. Not today or tomorrow. Not until Paris. This time is for you and I. You almost died two days ago and it makes me want to remind you how to live. Forget the bet, *querida*. For the next two days, here in this town, we'll be the best of friends. *Without* benefits. You want to see this city—I can see it in your eyes. So we'll go out. Eat delicious Catalan food that will make your mouth water. Enjoy the sun. See the sights and have some well-deserved fun.'

He truly wanted that, he realised. Just to feel like a man again—a man out with a beautiful woman and no cares in the world.

'What do you say?'

Violet-blue eyes—narrow with cynicism—peeked over the top of her sunglasses. 'I sense a subplot.'

With a chuckle he shook his head. 'Must you be so suspicious?'

She glared at him with a pensive pout. 'I'm not having sex with you, Nicandro.'

He peeked over *his* sunglasses and gave her a sinful wink. 'You keep telling yourself that, *bonita*.'

Pia *did* tell herself that, until it became a mantra in her mind and a torrid persecution in her body.

Nic was like a child with a new toy, and her suitcases had barely hit the floor of his palatial penthouse before he was dragging her down the frenetic La Rambla, strolling through the medieval alleyways and secluded squares of the old city, lyricising about every madcap Gaudí façade. Copious café's dotted the avenues, and she drank oodles of vanilla latte—espresso was Nic's poison—and paused to listen to the buskers, watch the pavement artists and be amazed at the living statues.

Pia adored every single minute of it. In fact she fell head over heels in love with the utter chaos and complete charm of it all.

Which just about described her new *friend* too.

Nic—or should she say tour guide *extraordinaire*—was amazing, with light-hearted mischief gleaming in his eyes as he spun her off in yet another direction. He was wonderful. Until the sight of her business suit sent him into an agitated state of incredulity.

'Don't you own any casual clothes, Pia? Anything that is not black?'

To which she haughtily responded, 'Black makes me look thinner.' Which, apparently, had been the wrong thing to say.

'That is the most ridiculous thing I've ever heard, Pia! I don't want you to look thinner, I want to see those glorious curves illustrated in colour!'

Pia considered the truth of that while she leaned against a drinking fountain in one of the squares, wincing at the pulsing sting of blisters on her heels and toes.

Meanwhile, Nic seemed to be having another fit—arms slashing in the air, frustration leaching out of him.

'Take them off, *querida*. I mean it. Look at your poor little feet! All squished.'

Down he went onto his knees in front of her with suave elegance and eased both shoes off her feet.

Pia frowned. 'What are you doing?' There was some fairytale about a shoe, she was sure.

'Playing Prince Charming.'

'Didn't he put the shoe *on*?'

He waved his hand in the air. 'Semantics.'

Then he grinned up at her—so utterly gorgeous—and shoved his sunglasses upwards to sit on his head, visor-like. She'd swear in any confession that her world tipped on its axis.

Wavy dark hair ruffled by the fingers of the breeze tumbled over his brow and curled around the upturned collar of his bright pink polo shirt. His white linen trousers were pulled tight over his spread thighs and she could see the thick ridged outline of his masculinity and remember the feel of it against her—

'Ohhh. That is *bliss*.' She drew the word out as if it had ten syllables as he pressed into the arch of her foot, banishing all thought. 'Keep going. More. *Harder*.'

He growled from his position between her legs. 'If you don't stop moaning in that smoky, sultry voice of yours I'll have you up against that wall over there and *harder* will take on a whole new meaning.'

Right now she'd probably let him. Spectacular—that was what he'd be. The thought should have shocked her, because sex didn't rate above 'okay' in her book.

Pia closed her eyes, tipped her head back and lost herself in his ministrations. No one had ever given her a foot-rub before—in fact it was the most selfless thing anyone had ever done for her. Those big hands were gentle yet firm, and the slow rub had her arching like a cat.

'*Dios*, look at you. This is torture. We have to move.'

No! Don't stop. 'Walk in my bare feet?'

'Hop on my back and we'll go to the boutique on the corner. I'm buying you new shoes and some decent casual clothes if it's the last thing I do.'

She wasn't sure which idea appalled her most. 'I can buy my own clothes, thank you very much, and there's no way I'm getting a piggyback into a exclusive designer store. How will *that* look?' The idea was preposterous.

He looked at her as if *she* was preposterous. 'Who cares? You might cut your feet otherwise, and you'll never get *those* back on.' He pointed to the offenders with a disgusted sneer, then spun around and lowered into an elegant crouch. 'Hop on.'

Pia swallowed hard as she eyed his wide shoulders. 'I can't believe I'm doing this,' she muttered, inching her skirt up her thighs and sneaking a peek to see who was watching. 'I weigh a ton. I could break your back.'

'You weigh one forty at the most, Pia. *Do it.*'

That commanding tone made her shiver. 'Fine. You asked for it.'

Hands hooked on his shoulders, she executed a graceless little jump and—thank God!—he caught her effortlessly, curling those big hands around her upper thighs as he stood tall.

'I like this,' he said, his thick, rich tone telling exactly how much.

Embarrassed beyond belief, she buried her face in his neck as he sauntered down the street, easy as you please, as if he did it every day of the week. It was all completely surreal. But the astonishing thing was her acute discomfort soon gave way to an odd bubbly feeling…maybe giddiness?…as people passed by and said things like, *Hola!* or *Bon dia!*, smiling at them as though they were sweet sixteen, madly in love and a delightful sight to behold.

And pretty soon she found herself smiling back and hanging on to Nic, her arms wrapped around his shoulders, wrists crossed on his chest, revelling in the feel of all his hard ridges and hot flesh. He felt glorious. Safe. Nuzzling his neck, she breathed in his earthy masculinity and felt his groan rumble up through his back and vibrate over her breasts.

'Good?' he asked.

Pia wasn't certain if he meant the feel of him, the smell,

or her lack of shoes, and decided the answer would be the same for all three. 'Divine.'

Another growl. Another deep rumble vibrating over her chest. And her heart thumped against the wall of her rib-cage. She was loving the effect she had on him. No matter what, that wasn't a lie or a secret, and she clung to that as tightly as she clung to him.

For so long he'd played the starring role in her tawdri-est fantasies—was it any wonder her resistance was slowly crumbling, leaving her to consider what would happen if she surrendered? Caved. Gave him his meeting. With Zeus. With *her*. Surrendered not only her body but also her true identity, her life. Not for a relationship—she wasn't *that* naïve, and in truth she wasn't interested in putting her heart on the line again for anyone, not after the humiliation of Ethan—but for one night in his bed.

One night of Nicandro Carvalho in exchange for risking it all. Would it be worth it? Probably not. Not to her. Not for sex. A fleeting pleasure versus losing Q Virtus. The old dinosaurs at the club would have her neck in a noose in no time if they knew a woman ruled their world. Heck, she'd only just managed to induct a number of serious-minded businesswomen into the fold, and that had taken her years. Dragging the place into the twenty-first century would turn her grey, she knew.

Rotten, stinking, filthy old laws.

But maybe he'll keep your secret, Pia. He knows about your past, virtually promised he'd tell no one. Maybe she could reveal herself. Trust him.

The infernal internal argument raged on, fuelling her anxiety and frustration. Too many maybes. Too many risks. Especially considering the rumours and the trouble at Eros.

But maybe she'd jumped to the wrong conclusions and he *had* just been looking for Zeus. She had no proof he was responsible apart from the fact that he'd broken into her office and had been snooping, but the more she knew of him the more she thought it was exactly the kind of risky, troublesome thing he'd do to find someone who, to be fair, was impossible to see. It didn't mean he was to blame for all her problems, did it?

Convincing yourself now, Pia? Maybe so, but if he wanted to cause trouble why save her life by holding her in his arms through the night? Why order her to sleep on the flight with fervent concern in his gaze? Why show her around the city and enjoy every minute? Massage her feet. Give her a piggyback so she didn't cut herself.

No. Just…*no.* It didn't fit. Any of it.

Lost in the tangled web of her thoughts, she didn't notice the glass plate frontage of the boutique until Nic came to a stop.

Pia wriggled to be let down. 'You can let go now.'

'I don't want to,' he said, with no small amount of petulance. 'I love feeling you against me, Pia.'

Whether it was his sincerity, the heat between them, or the gruff repressed need in his voice, she wasn't sure but she dipped her head and kissed him open-mouthed on the soft skin beneath his ear.

'Thank you for the ride, big guy.'

It had been considerate and caring and he needn't have done it. Who could blame her for being confused? This wasn't the man she'd met in Zanzibar—the calculating wolf who doubtless had an agenda. This man felt real. And, God help her, she wanted him. Wanted to trust him with everything she was.

Nic loosened his hold and she dropped to the warm stone pavement. Then he spun around, cupped her face and kissed her back tenderly, affectionately, on the mouth.

'Any time, *bonita.*'

As soon as they stepped over the threshold the store assistants were all over him like chocolate syrup—even the browsers couldn't take their eyes off him. Not that she blamed them. *And I've kissed him!* A startled thrill washed over her—the kind she hadn't had in for ever. *I've kissed him and I want to do it again. And again.*

Within half an hour Nic had packed her off to the changing rooms with a pile of clothes and Pia tore off her fitted jacket and skirt. The only way she could describe how she felt in that moment was free. As if her suit had been made of steel and she'd never known it. Eyeing the pile, overwhelmed and not sure where to even start, she heard a child-like whoop, knew it had something to do with Nic, and pulled the curtain aside to spy.

Standing on one leg, he balanced a dark red and blue Barcelona football on top of his elevated sneakered foot and held it there for long moments for the rapt attention of a young boy. After a while he gave a little kick, and Pia's jaw dropped as he started bouncing that ball over and over again. Never dropping it once. A back-kick and it was balanced on his nape with an expertise that had the entire store mesmerised. A second later he was nudging it a few inches into the air with his head repeatedly—she thought they were called headers but, hey, she'd never been into football…she could be wrong—and the young boy was grinning and clapping and cheering with utter delight.

Pia felt a silly smile on her face and her heart began to float in her chest. Before she knew it, snapshots of impossible dreams flashed in her mind.

He would be a wonderful father.

After a childhood of no authority, no order, no harmony, Antonio Merisi's controlled world had appealed to her so much she would have done anything to stay with him. And she had. But, looking back, it had been much like going from anarchy and chaos to despotism. A kind of tyranny.

Nic, on the other hand, was a glorious fusion of chaos and control. He could be commanding and dominant one minute, mischievous and wickedly sexy the next. As a daddy he'd be firm when he had to be, but probably the first to climb the nearest tree or jump in a nearby lake. And in that moment she envied the woman who would share that life with him.

An almighty shattering—like the sound of a hideously expensive vase being knocked off a shelf by a wayward football—splintered throughout the store.

Nic cringed so deeply his eyes squeezed shut. The little boy snorted, earning a glare from his mama. And Pia? She slapped a hand over her mouth to stop her giggle ripping free. And since when did she giggle? *Ugh.*

Contrite, Nic shrugged those big shoulders and smiled crookedly, almost blushing as he apologised to the staff. Pia honestly didn't know why he bothered, because they were all in love with him and he could have trashed the shop for all they cared. He could buy the place fifty times over and they knew he'd pay his dues.

After discarding a few outfits that she wouldn't be seen dead in, she settled on a sheer white T, a pair of jeans, a glamorous loose-fitting blazer and the softest pair of suede boots that made her feet sing. Then, before she could second-guess herself, she started to pull out the pins in her hair. Would Nic like her hair down? Even when she'd been sick it had stayed pinned back, so he'd never seen it—probably didn't know it was so long. Heck, maybe he wouldn't even care.

What's happening to you, Pia? What is he doing to you?

By the time she'd squashed her self-doubt, pulled the curtain back and stepped out, Nic and his partner in crime were sitting on the floor, leaning against the wall, chattering about the greatest football players of all time.

Pia cleared her throat. 'Are you boys behaving yourselves?'

Two faces jerked up. Two mouths—one big, one small—dropped.

'Wow. She's pretty. Is she your girl?'

Now it was Pia's turn to blush scarlet. Heat spread up her cheeks as Nic just sat there. Blinking. Staring.

Eventually he launched to his feet. 'I would like her to be. Do you think she should?' he asked the boy.

'Totally. You're cool.'

'This is my thinking exactly,' he said, with an arrogant nod that made her roll her eyes.

Pia watched him prowl towards her and covered up her unease by cocking her hip. 'Ta-da! Whadaya think?'

'I think that mouth of yours was made for better things than to speak slang, *querida*.' He walked around her, eyeing every curve, every nip, every inch. 'And I think you look ridiculously young, amazingly cute, a whole world lighter and the most beautiful woman I've ever seen.'

'Oh.'

'Speechless? *Dios*, has the world ended?'

'Sometimes I crave kicking you in the shin.'

From behind, he whispered huskily in her ear. 'Let's not get into cravings. Mine would make your toes curl and they are becoming more and more impossible to ignore.'

At the touch of his palm cupping her behind, she melted into a puddle.

'Your lush derrière was made for jeans—you know that?'

Oh, God. Then she felt him toying with a thick lock of her hair, the tug on her scalp sending her dizzy.

'You've finally unpinned your glorious hair. *Dios*, Pia, what are you trying to do to me?'

I'm not sure. Make you want me for me—not for who I am or what I can give you. Show you I'm more than the siren you want in your bed. Make you see me.

When he'd come full circle she stared at his mouth and he grinned wickedly.

'Want a taste, Pia?' he said, in that luscious, growly voice that made her tummy flip and her heart do a triple-somersault in her chest.

So of course she changed the subject. 'Where did you

learn to play football like that? You could've been a professional.'

It was as if she'd caused a power cut. The lights flickered. Blanked out. Then the stark flare of anguish in his eyes was so strong Pia had to root her feet to the floor to stay upright. What did they say about hidden depths? She'd never seen that kind of pain in him before. That depth of emotion.

'Nic? What did I say?'

Pain morphed into something hard and cold that made her shiver. But as quickly as it had come, it was gone.

'I was a pro. A long time ago.'

Oh, God, no wonder. 'So what happened?' she asked softly.

Turning his back on her, he stalked towards the cashier's desk. 'Injury. Let's go.'

She wanted to ask him how and why and when, but something told her he'd clam up even further because it would be opening a Pandora's box.

How awful that must have been for him. Having his dreams ripped away. And they *had* been dreams—no one could have missed the joyful, almost wistful smile on his face as he'd performed for the little boy.

Nic paid the bill after he'd given her a warning glare not to argue—in truth she'd never had anyone buy her a gift, and today had been so special she didn't want to bicker—and then asked for all the boxes to be delivered to his penthouse at the hotel. There seemed to be far too many, but she was so distracted with thoughts of his shattered aspirations she didn't question it.

When they'd left the store Nic reached for her hand, and this time Pia took it. She'd avoided his hold all day, but she had the distinct impression he was asking for comfort.

His strong, warm grip tightened, as if he were pleased, but once they were sauntering down the tree-lined avenue he flipped back to his jovial rakish self.

'Now we can hit the town,' he said. 'Dinner and a club—our first date.'

Pia stumbled on an invisible crack in the stone. 'Date? Do friends go on dates?' She couldn't even bear to think of her last date. It made her feel physically sick.

He placed his hands on her waist to steady her and cocked an eyebrow knowingly. 'Friends who want nothing more than to rip each other's clothes off? All the time.'

'There'll be no clothes-ripping tonight.'

Absolutely not. Here she'd been, unravelling at the seams, and he'd just reminded her of a time when giving her trust to a man had royally stitched her up.

His whisky eyes sparkled down at her and her stomach did a hot, sultry roll.

'You keep telling yourself that, *querida*.'

She *was*, dammit, and it didn't seem to be working a jot!

CHAPTER TEN

DUSK HAD PUNCHED through the day in a bruised swirl of rouge and the same violet-blue as her eyes, and the air was sharp-edged with salt from the Balcaric Sea.

She'd gone quiet, Nic mused, drawn inwards with a small pensive frown, and the only reason he could think of was the way he'd given dinner the innocuous title of a 'date.'

Still, he held her hand in his warm grip, unwilling to let go, knowing full well they were coming off as two inseparable lovers, and ushered her into the best tapas bar in town: a tiny undiscovered hole-in-the-wall discerning locals flocked to.

He leaned in and gave her arm a nudge. 'You have been on a date before, haven't you?'

Dios, she must have. Look at her. Those jeans made the blood rush to his head and his groin, making him simultaneously dizzy and hard.

'Casual' suited her to perfection. While he lusted after the sexy siren in power clothes, this was a softer look that gave her a girl-next-door vibe and made her so approachable that strangers thought nothing of striking up a conversation whenever they paused. A world away from Finnmark, where she'd been the high-class businesswoman in total control, verging on anally retentive, who'd had everyone on tenterhooks trying to anticipate her next move.

'Of course I have,' she scoffed—a tad defensively, in his opinion. Not many dates for Pia, then. Interesting.

While she snapped her spine pin-straight and hiked up her chin Nic laughed inwardly. If she thought those dense ice walls would perturb him she had another think coming.

'Nicandro! It has been too long, *amigo*!'

He grinned at the sight of Tulio Barros, the best chef on the planet, dark, short and sharp, with a wicked taste in art. 'It certainly has, my friend. Glad to see the place hasn't changed.'

The bar's main wall was a pastel canvas of tasteful yet evocative nudes from a bygone era, while the other three remained exposed brick. The rich scents of tapas baking, the dark wood slab tables and heavy chairs, the cream tiled floor—all lent the intimate space the warmth this part of the world was famous for. Nic loved it; somehow it reminded him of home, of Brazil, a place he hadn't visited in twelve long years.

The conversation exploded into a bout of, 'How have you been? How is business? Who is this beautiful lady?' and Nic curled his arm around Pia's waist and made introductions.

He could literally feel the tension ease from her body as Tulio soaked her in his Spanish charm and pointed to a small private table in the corner. 'Go sit at my table and I will bring some Sangria and my best dishes of the day, yes?'

Pia weaved through scattered handbags and chairs and eyed the seating.

Nic gave her another nudge. 'Trying to work out how to sit the farthest away from me?'

She pursed her lips. 'Yes.'

He chuckled darkly, getting a kick out of her blatant honesty. 'Something I will never allow. *Sit*.'

With a gorgeous little glare she slid along the bench and Nic followed, until they sat in the corner at right angles, knees bumping, flesh touching and Nic in his element, with a perfect view of the room and her beautiful face aglow from the intimate lighting.

Tulio poured tall glasses of Sangria—which she sucked through a straw, her full lips working rhythmically—and the man went all-out to tease her out of her shell with creamy squid rings, known as *chocos*, *patatas bravas* with creamy *alioli*, *llonganissa* sausage and *tigres*—stuffed mussels to die for.

Nic wanted to let loose a string of Brazilian curses as his trousers became too tight for comfort. He knew he was staring but, *hell*, she ate as if she was making love to her food. As if she savoured and gloried in every delicious morsel. And it was the most provocative sight he'd ever seen.

Those little licks, the slow, erotic roll of her tongue, watching her cheeks concave as she drank deeply—it all had him in a state of agony, with a hard-on that just wouldn't quit and a craving for her to take him inside the hot cavern of her mouth. It was killing him.

He tried to think of the last time he'd had no-holds-barred sex for hours on end, but all he could remember were some awkward dates and some passable yet mediocre sex. After that he'd told himself it just wasn't worth the hassle.

He'd meant to ask how many dates she'd been on—continuing their earlier conversation—but the nibbles and tentative bites and succulent licks were messing with his brain.

'How many lovers have you had?'

As for that steel band around his chest, tightening as he waited for her answer…? That was *not* jealousy or insecurity or obsessive behaviour. He simply needed to eat. When he ceased being riveted by her.

But this, apparently, had been the wrong thing to ask when her mouth was otherwise engaged.

Choking on a mussel, she lurched forward, and Nic rapped on her back until she could breathe without turning blue.

'Are you trying to kill me? That is none of your business!'

He gave her back a sympathetic rub and leaned closer to murmur in her ear, 'Which means none. Are you a virgin, *bonita*?'

'No!' Half the restaurant's patrons whipped their heads their way and she thumped his thigh under the table with her fist. Then she whispered furiously, 'For pity's sake, have you ever heard of a twenty-eight-year-old virgin?' Snapping upright, back pin-straight, she sniffed—a tad haughtily, if you asked him. 'I've had lovers.' Yeah, definitely defensive.

'Good lovers or mediocre orgasms at best?'

Jaw slack, eyes enormous, she shook her head at him. 'Do you have *any* filter between your brain and your mouth?'

'Mediocre, then. Hmm.' He brushed his fingers over his lips and smiled inwardly when he caught her staring and she licked her own pout. 'Why do you think that is?'

Had to be control. Pure and simple. He didn't believe in any of that garbage about there being 'The One' with whom sex was not just great, or even fantastic, but *life-changing*. How could sex be life-changing? What ludicrous hogwash. As for Pia… Come to think of it, he remembered how she'd frozen on the verge of her climax back in Finnmark. He knew the signs. He'd never left a woman unsatisfied in his life.

'You'll never experience earth-shattering, cosmic, star-realigning pleasure until you give up control. *Always* you have to be in control, Pia. If you let go the power of ecstasy you feel will be fifty-fold. You stopped yourself back in my cabin, didn't you?'

A hot flush slashed across her cheeks. *Busted.*

'I know a woman close to the edge, *querida*. If I had touched you where you were wet and wanting me you would have exploded.'

Darts of pique shot from her eyes, the violet deepening to the colour purple. '*Wow,* Nic, it's a wonder you can get that head of yours through the door. I just don't think I'm made for it. It's nothing to get excited about for me.'

Dios, no wonder she'd resisted him this long. '*"It"* being sex? You *can* say it, Pia. It's not illegal or immoral in this country.'

'Good job, since you'd have been convicted ten times over. Worldwide.'

She stuffed a meatball in her mouth and—call him a masochist—he followed every move.

'Strange that *innocent* would never be a word I'd think of with you but often that is exactly what you seem. You need educating, Pia.'

'And I suppose you'd be the man for the job, right? You'd make it your civic duty to ensure Olympia Merisi experienced a good orgasm?'

His face was a veritable invitation to debauchery in that moment, he knew. 'Ah, *querida*, I promise you there'd be *way* more than one—and "good" wouldn't even come close.' Nic leaned forward, dipped his head and drizzled whisper-soft kisses up the curve of her jaw before murmuring in her ear, 'By the time I was finished with you, you wouldn't know which way was up.'

Those gorgeous breasts began to heave as she struggled to suck in air.

'I think you've been hanging around ego-inflators too much, Nicandro. You really shouldn't believe everything women tell you. Money is the greatest aphrodisiac, and it makes the most expert liars.'

Her voice was more ice than fire, and the cold front washing over him prickled his skin.

Slowly Nic straightened as a lightbulb switched on and flooded his mind, illuminating every aspect of Pia with new meaning. Moreover, he'd have to be blind not to notice the pain that pinched her brow. Hell, he could virtually see her praying that he wouldn't jump on her *faux pas*.

'Let me guess. Some cad broke your heart, Pia?' It was pure conjecture but she was ripe pickings for anyone who knew her father. Heiress that she was. 'I imagine men are either intimidated by you or they're after your father's money. Is that about right?'

A heart-wrenching combination of reluctance, hurt and rage darkened her eyes and punched him in the gut.

'You could say that,' she said, in that hard, icy tone he hadn't heard for days and frankly had never wanted to hear again.

Now he understood the frozen façade a little better. Once bitten twice shy. Cliché, but true.

'What happened, Pia?' he asked gently, knowing it was a bad idea to push but incapable of stopping himself. He didn't like the idea that some man had damaged her, and that didn't bode well in light of his grand plan.

She stroked the smooth skin between her eyebrows in that way she did when she was deliberating. Unsure. Then she seemed to come to a decision, because she jerked up her chin and nailed him on the spot.

'I dropped my guard for no more than a minute. I believed every lie that came out of his mouth. I came to trust him. Then one night we went out on a date and I heard him telling his friends he was bedding Zeus's daughter to get into Q Virtus, and she was so easy he could marry her tomorrow and have the world at his feet.'

Nic's stomach took a nose-dive. No wonder she was holding back, defiant, rebelling against the insane biological chemistry between them. She'd been used, and the fact was in her eyes Nic was using her too—for a meeting. Wasn't he? Of course he was.

He tuned back in to her brittle voice. 'And do you know what my father said to me? He said, "Trust no man, Olympia. They all have an agenda. You want people to take a *woman* seriously? You stop acting like a whore.'"

The way she said *woman*—as if it was something to be ashamed of—rang alarm bells in his head. Hell, no, he wasn't having this—and it had nothing to do with any deal.

'Enjoying making love and being close to a man doesn't make you a whore, Pia. You have so much beauty stored inside you, and if you don't stir it up and let it flow out it will wither and die. Sex—making love—makes you feel alive. There's nothing to be ashamed of about that.'

The delicate curve of her throat convulsed. 'Are you saying this as a man who needs me in his bed to gain an audience with Zeus, or as a *friend*,' she taunted, reminding him of his words. 'A friend without benefits.'

'A friend. I promise you.' Oddly enough, it was the truth. 'Forget who I am or why we're here, sharing one another's company and great food. Do *not* let your past ordeal with a man dictate a future of a cold, solitary life. Was he your last lover?'

'Yes,' she said quietly, distractedly, as she glanced around the room, her gaze bouncing from one loved-up couple to another almost wistfully.

Nic swallowed hard, reached for her hand on the table and wrapped his fingers tight around hers, squeezing until he had her full attention. 'Keeping your distance, holding people away from you, denying yourself affection and a loving touch doesn't make you stronger, Pia. If anything it makes you weaker, because you're doing it out of fear.'

Her blonde brows drew down into intent little Vs, as if what he was telling her was far beyond mentally taxing. That over-active, constantly analysing brain of hers would be her downfall, he was sure.

'You're a beautiful, sensual woman, Pia, not meant to be alone. There's so much fire inside you. No matter what happens between us, promise me you'll remember that.

Be open to trying again. Not all men are dishonest, lying philistines and…' Nic trailed off.

I'm not either, he wanted to say, but that would be a barefaced lie. At least to her. Ironic that the one woman he wasn't being honest with was the one he wanted most.

Suddenly he felt as if someone had just picked him up and torn him clean down the middle. He wanted to crush the fool who'd bruised her heart, but he was about to do the exact same thing. Take advantage of her name, of who she was, exploit her for his own ends, use her just as badly as her last lover had.

Settling back in his seat, Nic closed his eyes, unsure if he could do it. Maybe he could find some other way to get to Zeus. *And what if you can't?* He was so close. After so many years he was now days away from facing the man who'd taken his parents from him, stolen his legacy, ruined his life.

Torn—so damn torn. Why was this tearing him apart? Why did he want her so badly? Why was he even considering her happiness before his own? His father's obsessive compulsions sprang to mind, but he squashed them just as swiftly. He was *not* his father!

Dammit, why was everything going so disastrously wrong?

Pia sat at the glass-topped table in Nic's penthouse, laptop open in front of her, gazing at the stunning sight of nightfall—a swollen waxy moon and a sky bursting with diamond-studded brilliance, its glow shimmering over a town that bustled with cosmopolitan chic glamour and frenetic energy.

Nic was backing off. Had been since the restaurant last night. The big seduction routine had crashed to a halt with the subtlety of a ten-car pile-up.

Often she caught him staring at her intently, with a voracious hunger that made her want to crawl out of her skin, but otherwise he was the perfect gentleman. Nic—*the perfect gentleman?* It was surreal. Maybe he'd been taken over by an alien life force or something. It was worrying to think he had such depth.

She'd half expected him to cancel their trip to the Picasso Museum that morning but, Nic being Nic, the idea hadn't seemed to cross his mind. Nor had cancelling tonight—their last night in Barcelona—and escorting her to his samba club in the old town. If someone had told her a month ago that she'd be sitting like some idiotic schoolgirl with a crush, counting down the hours, she'd have told them they were mentally insane. Yet here she was. Verging on lunacy.

Except no other man had ever looked at her the way Nic did. Predatory. Hungry. Just the heat in his whisky-coloured gaze, running hotly over her skin, their flames dancing in the dark depths like a physical manifestation of the blazing inferno that continued to rise up between them had Pia willing to do anything and everything he desired.

The bing-bong of an incoming e-mail diverted her attention to her mailbox.

No news. Nothing to link Carvalho to the hype at QV. He looks clean. Know more when I've spoken to PI in the morning.
Be careful, Pia.
J.

Careful? Wasn't she always careful? Always playing by the rules, using her head, emotionally barren. But with Nic she felt every sensation as if her senses were torn open and raw. As if she'd been held under the power of sensory deprivation her entire life—and maybe she had.

Her thoughts were severed by the ping of the elevator and the sight of Nic—all sweat and ripped muscle—coming back from his run.

Heaven help her, one look and her body simultaneously sighed in relief and flamed with heat, like some primal animal seeing her mate.

His hair was damp, the thick waves plastered to his brow. Beads of sweat dripped from his temples and clung to his chiselled jaw. And she could just imagine those corded, flexing muscular arms and his thick, powerful thighs moving with athletic grace as he pounded the pavement.

He scratched the hard ridges of his belly absently as he sauntered over, his dark gaze searing, as if he'd missed her face. 'Working again, *querida*?'

'Some problems at the club.' Pia looked at him closely but he didn't flinch at the mention of Q Virtus.

'Let your father deal with it, Pia,' he said, brisk and decisive.

She almost told him she didn't have that option.

'We'll leave in twenty minutes. I'm taking a quick shower.'

Can I be a fly on the wall?

Honest to God, he was sex incarnate, and the thought of another night lying alone in his huge bed in the guest room, thinking of how he'd made love to her mouth, how his thick hardness had nuzzled against the apex of her thighs, was a new form of persecution.

One hand on his hip, he didn't move an inch towards the shower, just stared at something beyond her left shoulder, and as she looked closer she could see stress bracketing his eyes. 'Is everything okay, Nic?'

Finally he met her gaze and his mouth shaped for speech, as if he wanted to tell her something. Something important, if his deep frown and tight jaw were anything to go by, and Pia felt as if she teetered on the edge of a cliff, waiting for a fall. His eyes lingered on her for long moments but he didn't answer her, didn't say a word, and after a frustrated clench of his fists he stalked off to the massive en suite bathroom.

Pia blew out a breath she hadn't known she was holding and slumped against the chair.

'By the way,' he said, loud enough to be heard through the penthouse. 'There's a box on your bed; you'll need it for the club tonight.'

There was?

Pia launched from the seat and tried not to dash through to her room like a child on Christmas morning. There on the pristine white sheets of the enormous four-poster bed was one of the boxes from the designer boutique; signature black, with a huge gold velvet sash tied into a sumptuous bow.

Her breathing grew a little fast and she rubbed her hands down her jeans.

A gift. Nic had bought her a gift. The man she'd watched from afar, the man who'd saved her life, the man who desired her like no other ever had. Surely this shouldn't feel so huge, so momentous, and yet that was exactly how it felt.

Arms wide, she curled her fingers under the lid and lifted, heart pounding with anticipation and excitement and the thrill of him doing something especially for her. Again.

Pia tossed the lid aside, looked down and sucked in air so fast her throat burned and tears stung the back of her eyes.

A red sheath lay on black tissue and with trembling fingers she stroked the embellished silk bodice and low-scooped neck, adoring the hand-stitched beads that tickled her palm. Lifting it from the wide straps, she noticed the fitted waist and the chiffon skirt that would kick out from her hips—a little flirty, a whole lot of fun—and flare out when she spun. It wasn't something she'd have chosen in a million years, but as she dressed in a daze, slipping the fabric over her head, letting the silk whisper over her skin and kiss her cleavage, for the first time in her life she felt like a billion dollars.

Odd how she could have bought hundreds of dresses just like this but had never wanted to—never had the need to dress up for anyone. But this… This dress was worth more than her fortune—at least to Pia—because it was a gift from the heart of a man who had to care. He *had* to.

And it was about time she admitted to herself that she cared right back. Had wanted him before they'd ever met face to face. Question was, did she have the strength to go for it? Surrender to him? Give him her body and reveal who she was? Take the ultimate risk?

Lost in thought, she lifted her left leg like a flamingo, reached down and nudged her foot into one glittering red stiletto. Then the other.

A quick glance in the mirror and she knew exactly what was missing.

Grabbing her jewellery case from the dark wood vanity, she slid the catch and opened the box, her heart doing a little pitter-patter as she spied the large black teardrop diamond and remembered the day her father had given it to her. No affectionate kiss on the cheek or words of love, but she'd known he'd cared for her in his own way and that had been enough. More than she'd ever expected or hoped for.

Lifting the chain from its bed of velvet, she watched the prisms from the chandelier above glint off the smooth black surface and the flash of a memory dimmed her buoyant mood. *Zanzibar*. The pure loathing in Nic's eyes had been strong enough to make her feel genuine fear.

Shivering, she gave a cursory glance towards the door to see if he was out of the shower, wondering if anything had been unearthed about Santos Diamonds. Then, to preserve her fragile optimism, she snapped the case shut. Maybe Nic truly *did* have voodoo suspicions about black jewels, and he was in a strange enough mood as it was.

When she stepped out into the hallway the sound of rushing water lured her towards the open doorway of his wholly masculine en suite bathroom.

Steam poured over the top lip of the towering glass enclosure, pluming in the air with moist heat, and when she took a tentative step closer her heart gave a pang at the sight of him. Ached so badly she could hardly stand it.

Arms braced on the black granite tile, head down as the water poured over him in a hot wet rush, he looked utterly torn. Frustrated. Demoralised.

As if sensing her presence, Nic lifted his head and twisted at the neck until she could see his profile. Water dripped down his nose and he wiped his face over his hard bicep to clear his eyes.

'Pia?'

He was so beautiful. From the hard sculpted lines of his back to the tapering of his waist, the dimples at the base of his spine and the perfect firm curves of his sexy butt.

Moisture dotted in between her breasts as her blood heated.

'Did you buy the dress before or after you smashed the place up?' she asked, her voice thready as she unravelled before him.

'Before I broke a two-thousand-euro vase? Yes. Do you like it? The dress?'

'I love it, Nic. Thank you.'

He gave a small nod. 'You're very welcome.'

She couldn't look away—could only imagine what it would be like to strip off his gift, walk in there and act out any of the various tawdry fantasies she'd conjured up over the past week. And all the while he didn't move a muscle, kept his body averted, and she started to ponder if he was thinking of her in the same way. If he was as turned on as she was.

'You need to leave…*now*.'

Her stomach twisted with pure and painful longing. 'What if I don't want to?'

Tipping forward, he banged his forehead off the wall and ground out, 'I'm not making love to you, Pia.'

The penny dropped. In fact it was as if she'd hit the

jackpot and all the nice shiny coins were pouring out in a gold rush.

He didn't want her to feel used. The way Ethan had made her feel. *Now* she understood. *Now* she wanted him more than ever. He would *never* purposely hurt her.

Pia smiled, but all she said was, 'You keep telling yourself that…*querido*.'

CHAPTER ELEVEN

'I'VE CHANGED MY MIND.'

At Nic's voice, Pia tore her eyes away from the limousine window and the sight of La Catedral, with its richly decorated Gothic façade graced with gargoyles and stone intricacies. Then she cursed inwardly.

One look was all it took tonight. Her lower abdomen clenched with want—empty, so needy she bowed slightly to ease the ache.

Nic put her in mind of a roguish prince in his wicked midnight-blue suit, with his unruly hair black in the dim light and curling seductively at his forehead and nape. He'd eschewed a tie in favour of an open collar and the sight of his smooth tanned throat was making her weak at the knees.

'About what?' she asked, cringing at the quiver in her voice.

'This is the most beautiful I've ever seen you.'

'You say that every time I change clothes.'

One side of his lush mouth kicked up. 'A man's prerogative, *querida*. Are you going to dance with me tonight?'

His voice, she noticed, was still thick and rich, but there was a hesitant tone there too and it matched his manner. As if he was so deep in thought, so conflicted, he was tearing himself apart. Clearly he didn't want to talk about it—she'd asked him often enough—but that didn't mean Pia wasn't listening.

'Yes, I want to dance. But I'll warn you now I have no idea how.'

'I can teach you the samba in five minutes. Or the rumba. Have a little faith—your body was made for dancing.'

The dark interior charged with an electric current that gave a sharp ping when Nic glossed his warm palm over her knee and drew tiny circles with his thumb over and over. A covetous touch that made her pulse spike. She wanted to feel him inside her so badly she could barely sit still. It was getting worse, she realised, this inescapable want. It was as if she just couldn't breathe without him touching her.

Squirming in her seat, she scrambled for something to say. 'This is *your* club we're going to?'

'Yes. Barcelona is one of my favourite cities in the world and a friend of mine—an actor, believe it or not—was bemoaning the lack of good dance clubs when he came into port. Next thing I knew I'd opened one. Una Pasion Hermosa—A Beautiful Passion.'

The car rocked to a stop outside a trendy upmarket nightclub with an endless queue and a dizzying red carpet.

Just like that her sangfroid flew out of the window. 'Good name. Is it a celebrity haunt?'

'Generally. Depends who's in town.'

The car door opened to the excitable cacophony of the crowd and Nic flowed from his seat—all sleek masculine elegance—and held out his hand.

She stared at it like an idiot, trying to ignore the nauseating curl in her stomach.

'Pia?'

Oh, God. Deep breath, hand in his and up she went, swirling into the foyer in a blur of blinking camera lights, ducking her head self-consciously, coming unglued with the idea that people would try and figure out who she was. Nic might be used to the limelight but she wasn't. She chose instead to stay behind the scenes. Very few knew her true identity and she wanted to keep it that way.

'Nic,' she whispered furiously. 'Maybe this isn't such a good idea. Won't people know you? Wonder who I am?'

He shrugged with so much insolence she could have whacked him. 'Only my staff really knows who I am, and they are paid very well not to make a fuss. They're used to high-end clientele and I doubt anyone will look twice at us.'

Nic wrapped his hand around hers tightly, as if sensing she was about to go nuclear with the power of angst-laced adrenaline rushing through her veins, and she felt the flow of tension drift from her body on a slow sweeping wave.

Come on, Pia. You don't want to ruin your last night fretting about things that might never be, do you? No. She wanted to enjoy every second. Live in the moment. Out in the real world. For once not hiding.

Nic led her to one of the private booths set on an elevated dais and Pia slid into the overstuffed velvet bench seat, feeling the seductive bass line of the Brazilian samba pound through her blood.

'What's your poison, Pia?' he said, leaning over, his whisky eyes aflame with heat and desire.

'You choose. I don't want to make any decisions tonight. I want to just…*feel.*' Her voice sounded unreal. Loose. Licentious. As if her body was slowly taking over the power of her analytical mind.

Nic ordered French 75s and they were delivered minutes later, served in champagne tulips. Pia blamed the heat for what she did next: knocked back the first gulp with so much abandon she almost blew her head off.

'Wow. Potent stuff. Someone just shot a flame-thrower down my throat.'

'For a potent lady,' he murmured, lips carved with a devilish smirk. 'A gutsy, lusty blend of gin, champagne, lemon juice and sugar.'

The way he puckered his lips and said *'sugar'*, with a

naughty, intoxicating lilt, sent the delicious tart-sweet cock-tail straight to her head. And all she could see was the swar-thy sexy mess of his dark hair, the lights flickering over his aristocratic face, the smooth bronzed skin of his throat.

Good God, this sensation of recklessness was like being on a brutally intense rollercoaster and she wanted the ride to go harder and faster, way beyond control.

When Nic caught her staring and raised an arrogant brow she tore her eyes away, more than a little perturbed at her complete lack of morals. Was she coming off as some kind of…? *Of what, Pia? Whore?*

No. No, she wasn't going there. What had Nic said? Being close. Affectionate. Yearning for a lover's touch. She'd never had that before. That was probably why it had made her feel so dirty to be used. She'd allowed Ethan to make her feel worthless. But this give and take, connec-tion and tenderness, had its own kind of beauty and there was nothing dirty about that—he was right.

Proof of that was in the crush of dancers moving sinu-ously across the floor to the unique samba beat. Under the brilliant strobes they were all beautiful arches and lines, weaving in light and shadow.

She focused on the couples who appeared to be lovers and picked up the nuances of their behaviour. The man tucking his lover's hair behind her ear, kissing her jaw-line, the tip of her nose, nuzzling her collarbone—all fiery heat, promising dizzying pleasure. More than anything she wanted to be close and affectionate like that with Nic.

'You're looking at them with such heart-shattering long-ing, Pia. What is going through that pretty head of yours?'

She didn't answer—couldn't…not with such a great lump in her throat.

'Maybe you are ready to dance, yes?'

'Now or never.' And she meant that literally. Something told her tonight was her last chance, her only chance with him, and if all she ever had was the heady sensation of his body moving against hers—even fully clothed—then so be it. She'd take it. It would be enough.

Pia stepped onto the pulsing dance floor and before she could think about where to stand or how to move Nic was there, taking control, taking the lead.

Aggressive, dominating, he curled his left arm around the base of her spine and pulled her to him, crushing her breasts against his chest. Then he clasped her right hand tightly in his—a silent declaration that he wouldn't let her fall, wouldn't let go. The moment was achingly wonderful, and as she looked up into his eyes and saw the longing reflected back at her she knew she was done for. Knew she'd never feel this way again.

'That's it, *querida*. Relax. Give all that control over to me.'

She had the notion they were talking about more than dancing, and she was already halfway to coming undone and unravelling quickly.

'Feel the contagious beat in your blood. Let the music move you; let it flow through your body and follow my lead.'

His voice was a giddy narcotic all on its own as he confidently steered her around the whirl of tight bodies and swaying hips.

Pia clutched his strong upper arms, loving the sensation of honed muscle beneath her fingers, and yet he bent them and moved with such masculine grace he was a stunning sight to see. His hands splayed across her lower back, where he gripped her tight and then moved their hips in a figure eight—all sensuality and sin—and then she was twirling like a top as he executed a perfect spin.

Just like that she was dancing, and she'd never felt so connected to another person in her entire life.

A second later she slammed back into his chest, palms flat, panting softly, breasts swollen and heavy, nipples peaking against the lace of her bra, begging to be touched.

Nic gazed down at her, all broody and dark.

It was like dancing with the devil, she realised. His every movement was a wicked invitation to vice, his covetous touch was possessed with danger, his scorching hot body created to spawn lust.

That was when she noticed. Nic wasn't the only one looking at her. Them.

'People are watching us,' she breathed.

'And most are obscenely envious of me, *querida*. Not to mention turned on.'

Well, they weren't the only ones.

His grip was firm but tender, holding her in the way a musician might prise the best from a rare instrument, and with every undulation, every sinuous return of her hips, her body hummed like a piano wire and she felt a hiccup of orgasmic pleasure. Not a full-on climax but a short, sharp, sweet jolt that was gone in an instant. Then another would hit, and suddenly she was shaking with uncontrollable need.

'Nic?' *Oh, God.* This was a whole new level of sexual tension.

Their bodies were so close from the waist up they barely moved. Her cheek now rested against his and the smell of his skin made her head spin, as if he was twirling her round and round the floor. When she inhaled through her mouth she could taste him, and her mind began to wander imagining a scene playing out...

Nic holding her down—wickedly naked—as they danced to an earthly wanton tune in his bed.

Dizziness hit her like a truck and the next thing she knew she was on her tiptoes, pressing her lips to his. *Kiss me, please.*

He hesitated and dread thrashed its monstrous tail, whipping her insides until—*oh, yes*—he thrust his hands into the fall of her hair and coaxed her mouth open with his tongue. Until she was seduced into an erotic play that had her nerves singing as he kissed her with such unrestrained passion she thought she might faint.

Beneath the mastery of his plundering lips the ache between her thighs grew to painful proportions full of emptiness and need. And impatience gathered inside her, right *there*, at the base of her abdomen, its frustrating heat spreading outward.

Pia undulated against him, stroking the thick erection that pushed against his seam over and over.

'*Dios*, Pia. You're killing me,' he groaned into her mouth, his hands unsteady as they moulded to her body.

His touch was electric and it seemed to be everywhere and nowhere all at once. She needed him to do something. To take control. Take *her*.

That was another thing he'd been right about. It was all about control for her, and she didn't like giving hers up. It made her afraid of being hurt. But in giving up her power and control to Nic, in return he'd give her something she needed far more right now. The assurance that what she had to offer of herself was worth giving to someone. That *Pia* was worth it. That her past hadn't tainted her beyond value.

'I want you, Nic. So much…' she whispered as she nuzzled across his jaw, and the last vestiges of doubt dissolved beneath the power of his searing heat. 'Take me back,' she implored. '*Take me.*'

So foolhardy. So reckless. So inevitable.

Emotion roamed across his features, shifting from conflicted to cautious to aroused and everything in between.

Pia watched the war raging inside him…

Then her heart smiled.

The limousine was dark. Streetlamps flashed at regular intervals, flaring through the shadowy black leather interior. And he tried to say no, to hold on, but within seconds of them tumbling into the car she was straddling his lap and gyrating against him. It was biological fireworks and he was only human, right? He'd been desperate for her since the day they'd met.

His agonising erection nudged the mound of her lacy briefs, pressing into her hot wet folds, and his mouth was on hers, ravenous, devouring, stunningly erotic.

For the first time in his life he was incapable of restraining his impulses—his body's carnal urges were stronger than his cast-iron will.

It was all hands and mouths and thrusting hips, murmured begging and endearments that made no sense, but they were both past the need to care about anything but pleasure and release.

The desire, already voluminous, became so acute he thought he was going to have a heart attack. How he was going to last the eight-minute drive was beyond him.

The sound of cloth tearing reached his ears, and when he felt her hungry hands on his chest he let out a low groan.

'Pia, slow down—or I swear you'll be on the floor in ten seconds flat.'

It seemed her version of 'slow' varied widely from his, because her open mouth glossed down his chest and licked over the flat copper disc of his nipple.

Nic hissed, but the sound was cut off when he felt her fingers at his waist, unbuttoning his trousers.

He should stop her, really. But, dammit, he didn't want to. Just wanted to feel her hot hands on him, her fingers wrapped around his pulsing thick length. Just. Like. *That*.

Nic's brain blew a circuit or two, but that didn't stop him from looking down. *Big* mistake. Her tongue snaked out and licked into his belly button before travelling down, down…

'Pia…' he growled with warning.

'I've wanted to do this since I saw you tied to my chair,' she said, in that smoky, sultry voice that drove him wild. Dropping soft, moist kisses down his length, she breathed hotly, 'Did you want me then? Think about me doing this?'

'*Dios*, yes—*yes*!'

Her hot wet tongue flicked and licked around the swollen head of him, the soft sensual pressure spiking his pulse and firing his blood. His every thought fragmented. Then her mouth opened wide and his vision blanked.

'*Pia...*'

He gritted his teeth as her lips slid down his erection on a soft suck, her tongue circling every sensitive nerve-ending.

Nic cried out, then bit his lip to stifle the sound. 'Pia... you need to slow...stop.'

Somehow his hand had taken on a life of its own and he weaved his fingers into her flaxen hair and gently thrust into the slick heat of her mouth, begging her to make love to him harder, faster, and he lost it—let his head fall back onto the cushioned leather and undulated, gasping at the wicked pleasure of it all.

What she was doing to him in the back of a limo...what people could see if the windows weren't tinted—Pia was driving him out of his tiny mind. And without warning it was all suddenly too much. Electricity charged his skin and his hair stood on end as his body tensed, the power rising like an unstoppable wave.

'Pia...too much... I'm going to... You need to move. *Now.*'

But she didn't move, only gave a tiny whimper and a groan of unadulterated pleasure that vibrated down his groin. And that was it. His entire body seized as his orgasm hit him like a crack of thunder, the sensation both unexpected and anticipated, and mind-numbing pleasure reverberated outwards, stealing his breath.

Heart pounding in his ears, his harsh rasping breath filled the stifling air as he scrambled for his brain to kick in.

When he figured he could talk again, or at least try, he swallowed. Hard.

'That was incredible. *You* are incredible.' Nic reached down and hauled her back into his lap, then buried his nose in her hair and clutched her to him. 'I want you naked and in my arms and in my bed. I want to hear your cries echo through the room, and it has nothing to do with any deal or bet or power-play. Screw the meeting, Pia, let us have this night.'

He'd find some other way to get to Zeus—without using her. He couldn't do it. He wanted something honest and real with her, and taking away their deal was the only way.

She eased back and the streetlights flickered over her exquisite face as he watched her confusion morph into a sweet kind of happiness.

'You mean it?' she whispered. Hopeful. Beautiful.

'Every word.'

With a glorious little smile she kissed him, soft and slow. It was almost shy, distinctly vulnerable, the way she needed to keep touching him.

Nic kept a tight hold of her, tasting himself on her tongue, luxuriating in a tender intimacy he'd never known. Especially after an act so sensually erotic. But then he'd known from the first that she would turn any idea in his head upside down and shake it up. She was unpredictable, and that was the one thing he loved and feared most about her.

His revived need was a living, breathing ball of fire, burning his patience to cinders, and he worshipped her, lavishing patient moist affection over every millimetre of soft, scented pearly skin he could reach.

Pia gripped his upper arms—each nail a brilliant half-moon of perfect agony—and just as he tilted sideways and rolled her onto her back across the wide seat the car shuddered to a stop.

'*Gracas a Deus*. Perfect timing.'

Hovering above her, Nic revelled in the way she arched her back and tipped her head in a non-choreographed compulsion of pure obedience. He knew exactly what she wanted—Nic to take control, to show her the kind of earth-shattering pleasure he'd promised.

Reaching up, she cupped his face and confirmed it. 'I want you so much, Nic. I want you to need me, take me, make me feel like you said I would.'

'No pressure, then.'

She laughed, the sound so glorious he knew there was no place he'd rather be—and that wasn't only astounding, it was terrifying.

'Just take it all away. Melt the ice inside me. Make me feel alive, just once.'

I want him. Need him so much. It was laughable, because as if any need this elemental was really a choice.

It was a beautiful, terrible desire—one she'd sworn she'd never let herself feel again. In truth, she could hardly compare what she had with Nic to her past—it was like water to wine—but it was a door that led to heartache. Not the loving kind but the using kind—the kind that made her feel cheap and worthless. So she'd sealed herself off, determined never to reopen herself. Yet here she was, opening up once more.

But he'd said no deal. That this was no game. To forget about tomorrow and live for tonight. If he wanted her that much it must mean something. *Had* to.

Tomorrow she'd give him Zeus and he would trust her. They would talk and together they'd find a way to figure it all out.

Pia was strung so tight the slightest pluck on her strings resonated, and when the elevator doors pinged shut she flinched. But Nic was right there, cinching her waist, lifting her up until she was level with his mouth and kissing her with thrust after languorous thrust of his tongue, licking into her mouth, taking her higher and higher, until she was a floating cloud of sensation.

'Wrap your legs around me, *bonita*, let me feel you.'

She did just that and ground her pelvis against him—
the aftershocks sending rippling shivers down her spine—
while she kneaded the hard ridges of his upper back.

Nic nuzzled down her throat, across the bare skin of her
chest, dropping moist, luscious kisses across the curve of
her breast where it swelled above her bodice, breathless
in his need.

'I need to see you.'

That was the only warning she got before he lowered
her to the ground and pushed the red satin straps off her
shoulders.

'I'm so hungry for you I could eat you alive.'

A dizzying pulse of excitement made it difficult to
think, but if any doubts lingered his answering passion
razed them to the ground.

In a red blur, fabric swished down her body and pooled
on the floor. And when Nic took a step back to gaze down
at her, displayed under the harsh light, she shook inside,
wanting to cover herself up. She wasn't as lithe as his usual
conquests, not so toned, not so sculpted, more soft and
generous.

'*Dios*, Pia, look at you. You take my breath away.'

Tentatively she lifted her chin, and what she saw in his
eyes melted the final shards of ice in her heart. Reverence.
Ferocious desire.

With one finger he reached out and drew a line from her
collarbone down the deep cleavage of her breasts—*thank
you, push-up lacy bra*—and farther still over the slight rise
of her stomach to the dip of her panties.

He let out a low rumbling groan. 'You're killing me,
here. Those sexy stockings and seams. I am keeping them
on, *querida*, and licking up every line. Turn around.'

The command in his voice was unmistakable—wrapped
in silk and satin and awe and tenderness, but there none-
theless.

Her panties sliced across her cheeks and she gave another little thank-you for bum squats as she gave him what she hoped was a seductive look from beneath her eyelashes and turned, arms spread wide, palms flat to the mirrored wall.

Never had she felt so confident, so provocative, so sexual, so insanely turned on.

'Heaven help me,' he growled. 'I think I've just come again.'

She laughed—she couldn't help it—and watched his reflection, the heat in his eyes, the desire that made her blood thicken in her veins. But there were other emotions there too. Affection, and a pride that made her giddy heart leap to her throat. For a moment she considered that this might mean far more to her than was wise.

Then he was on his knees and fulfilling his promise—kissing up her stocking seams, his lips as soft and teasing as the touch of a feather—and she trembled where she stood.

Her hot panting breaths steamed the mirror and she watched her own eyes grow heavy and slumberous as he went higher, higher…reaching the bare pinch of skin where her thigh met her bottom.

'Nic?' Tremors ran up her legs and gathered at the soft folds of her femininity. Her inner walls clenched with an unbearable need for something inside. Nic inside her. Filling her up. Making her whole. 'Please.'

He nudged her legs wide and she cursed the stilettos making her teeter as his dextrous fingers slipped forward to stroke her where she was hot and wet and— 'Oh, my God, Nic!'

'So close,' he murmured, kissing the nape of her neck. 'But I won't let you come yet, Pia. I forbid it. You have to wait until I'm deep inside you.'

'I hate you,' she whispered adoringly.

His dark chuckle was interrupted by the *ping* of the elevator doors and the sharp noise was the final pluck on her nerves. Her legs buckled beneath her.

'Whoa, *bonita*. Oh, no, you don't.' Nic swept her into his arms, held her against his chest and strode into the penthouse, down the hall to his bedroom—where he laid her in the centre of his huge satin-drenched bed.

She writhed in pleasure as his gaze soaked up her sumptuous black bra, skimpy chiffon panties and stockings.

'Now, *that* is a picture I will never forget,' he said, his voice thick with passion as he stripped in front of her, shameless in his skin.

Those hot eyes were burning, threatening to incinerate her where she lay breathless, waiting for his muscled physique to come into view.

He was so fabulously tall that from her position on the bed she felt as if she was staring up at the cathedral in the square.

Lascivious and wolfish, the smile on his mouth was as heady and thrilling as the need etched tightly across his gorgeous face. And the last vestige of her sanity went the way of his snug hipsters when he took himself in his hand, circled his fingers and brushed his thumb across the head of his erection in a way that made the air whoosh out of her lungs.

He was winding her up like a musical toy, and the coiling tension became so acute she almost feared the inevitable striking chorus of release.

Softness came up to swallow her back as hardness descended from above and she found herself sandwiched between heaven and hell.

'What am I going to do to you first, *querida*?' He unlaced the ribbon bows of her panties, tied at her hips, and tugged the lace free.

Just the pull of the fabric against her folds tore a whimper from her throat. She didn't care what he did as long as he did *something*.

'I think you are too close for more play, Pia,' he growled as he lavished her with more kisses across her collarbone, up her throat.

Pia twisted, nuzzling his face to find his mouth, and at the first thrust of his tongue between her lips her heart pitched.

She strained towards him, canting her hips, bowing her whole body, while her emotions whiplashed from wanton desire to wholehearted devotion. 'Make love to me like you promised,' she begged. 'Please, Nic. *Please.*'

'*Dios,* Pia, you are on fire. Burning up.'

He pushed her down into the mattress, pinned her beneath his body, his hands forming sweet warm shackles about her upper arms, and pushed inside her in one long, hard, powerful thrust. And—*oh, yes!* She revelled in the wicked slide into oblivion.

Their eyes locked—his stunned whisky depths meeting awestruck violet-blue—as they shared one breath, the moment so profound she wasn't surprised to feel a tear escape the corner of her eye.

Right then it occurred to her that she'd just made a fairly spectacular misjudgement. One night would never be enough and she'd dream of this man always.

Gazing down at her, Nic brushed damp hair back from her forehead and the tenderness of the gesture wrenched her already wide open heart. So she turned her face to hide in the crook of his neck and breathed deeply.

'No, Pia, don't do that. Don't hide from me. Not tonight.'

'I…' *I need you.*

As soon as she obeyed him and glanced back up he began to move—slow and shallow at first, teasing her to a cataclysmic high—until she was writhing beneath him and his thrusts became deeper, harder, more powerful than anything she'd ever known. Until where Nic ended and she began was the ebb and flow of an erotic wave of pleasure.

She wanted to touch his skin, feel the flexing muscle of

his ripped body beneath her palms, but those sweet warm shackles only moved upward to hold her wrists above her head with one of his large hands. The other skimmed down her cheek, farther down her throat and over her chest, to cup her breast and squeeze the aching flesh.

A desperate moan blistered the air—his or hers, she wasn't sure, didn't care—as he rubbed over her nipple, then sucked the tight peak into his hot mouth.

'Nic… Nic…' She chanted his name over and over and it seemed to fuel his inner fire. Not to move faster but to slow, as if he knew she was close and wanted to prolong the agonising pleasure.

'One more minute—then I will let you fly.' His voice shook, his hands were unsteady from holding himself back, and she realised he was in as much pain as she was.

'Nic…*please.*'

'So beautiful,' he murmured, still moving at that maddening pace, keeping her on the edge of a shattering fall.

Pia dipped her chin, silently begging for his mouth, and he gave her what she wanted—*needed*—and simultaneously thrust his tongue into her mouth and slammed his hips forward with a tiny undulation that rubbed her sweet knot of nerves once…twice…

'Nic!'

'Now you may come. *Now.*'

Lightning bolts of sensation gathered in her core like a bright white pinpoint of light—a star about to go supernova—and the cry that tore from her throat felt wrenched from her soul.

Bursts of pleasure shot outward and those streaks of lightning tore down her spine and crackled along her nerves with an almost spiteful ferocity—the sheer intensity stealing her breath and holding her on an erotic plateau that made her vision blank, her mind faze out and life cease to exist for long, endless moments.

She came to as Nic released the shackles from her body

and soul and rose above her, chasing his own nirvana. He captured her lips in a deep kiss that was tinged with desperation. Held her with a reverence she'd only ever dreamed of, making her feel accepted and worthy and wanted beyond reason. So perfectly *herself* that falling was inevitable.

His cries were wrecked and ravaging as his orgasm tore him apart and Pia licked at his lips to taste his pleasure—pleasure *she* had given him—ecstasy he'd found only in her.

His glorious weight descended and she felt safe and cared for, and cherished in the crush. And she knew it was coming—was powerless to stop it.

The overwhelming cacophony of emotions—joy and fear and adoration and amazement—refused to be ignored, and they rose up within her and escaped in a breath suspiciously close to a sob. Nic gathered her in his arms and held her with fierce strength—stronger than a mighty god. Almost devout. It was the culmination of such an amazing night that she wished she could freeze the moment in time for ever.

CHAPTER TWELVE

WHO'D HAVE THOUGHT Nicandro Carvalho was a cuddler?

Pia smiled, reminiscing about the way he'd followed her around the bed like a heat-seeking missile. When he hadn't been making love to her, that was. One minute he could be deeply intense and dominating, his lovemaking so powerful it wrought tears, and the next he was light-hearted and fun, making her laugh out loud with teasing touches and that wicked, incorrigible grin. He thought nothing of saying something outrageous mid-thrust as he took her against the wall or pleasured her on his knees. She'd never imagined couples could make love in so many different ways. But, then again, maybe that was just Nic. Maybe only he could be like that.

The high of the night still rushed through her veins but there was a dark cloud closing around her, obscuring her euphoria, obliterating her joy. It was over. Time to get back to the real world, check on work, unveil the truth and tell Nic exactly who she was.

Pia eased from his hold and slipped from the bed with a slight wince, deliciously sore and tender. She told herself not to look back, only forward. Yet still she couldn't resist one glance at the sheets that held the impression of their lovemaking and the beautiful tall, dark man who'd taken her to heaven.

Heart heavy, she snuggled into a soft fluffy robe and wandered into the kitchen for her early dose of caffeine.

Ten minutes later she sat at the glass-topped table, coffee in hand, her laptop open at the financial section of a Saturday newspaper.

Eros had taken another kicking, she noticed, feeling the punch of it in her stomach and an after-ache of dread.

Pia flipped through the pages to check Merpia. Looked okay. Back to the stock exchange…flick, flick, flicking the pages—

Her fingers stilled on the keys. She backed up—heart thumping—sure she'd seen his name… *Nic's name…there.*

Goldsmith stock climbs as a merger in matrimony with real estate magnate Nicandro Carvalho is revealed.

What?
Fingers now flying, Pia jumped from one site to another through various links, with a sickening fear that instead of being poised for flight into a brave new world, she'd propelled herself well past the edge, no wings in sight, and was about to plunge into a black void that would swallow her whole.

Somehow she ended up in the New York society pages, her throat so tight she couldn't breathe, her heart beating so hard and fast she could barely see, let alone read the words.

Carvalho out and about in Barcelona with a mystery blonde.
Goldsmith heiress leaving the Fortuna mansion under cover. Hiding tears?
Billionaire Nicandro Carvalho at his nightclub in Barcelona with a new playmate. Who could she be?

'Oh, my God,' she breathed, her fingers fluttering over her mouth, the tears scorching the backs of her eyes making the hideous photograph of her and Nic distorted and blurred. She looked like a tramp. She looked like the whore her father had told her she was—and, goddammit, she felt like it!

And that girl—the girl Nic was apparently marrying—looked genuinely devastated as ravenous newshounds circled her, ready to catch her fall on candid camera. Suddenly Pia was grateful for them, because she'd ignored the truth, convinced herself there was more between them. Instead she'd fallen under his spell, surrendered herself to him body and soul during his magnificent last act.

Hadn't she learned *anything*? Had the past taught her *nothing*? She was only good enough to use. Worthless for anything more.

Pia slammed the laptop down, bolted upright, sending the chair screeching across the floor, and stormed through the living room, headed for his bedroom, furiously brushing at her tears because she would *not* cry in front of him— she would not.

The shrill of her phone cast her to stone. The phone she'd been ignoring most of the night. Something she'd never, *ever* done before.

She didn't have to look at the caller. She didn't have to greet Jovan or say a word. Because in that moment she might not know the *why* but she certainly knew the *who*.

'Pia? Tell me you got my message—tell me you are *not* still with him.'

Self-loathing so thick she almost choked on it. Humiliation so sharp she almost cut herself on it. Pain so powerful it almost crushed her bones. Heartbreak so shattering she could hear her soul weep.

She could barely breathe for hating. Herself or Nicandro Carvalho, she wasn't sure.

'Pia, are you there? I still cannot believe he is alive. I was *there*, Pia. At the Santos mansion. I was *there*! Where are you, dammit?'

'In bed with the enemy. Am I not?'

CHAPTER THIRTEEN

Eiffel Tower—Monday six p.m.
Zeus will be there.

THAT HAD BEEN her goodbye. The only lingering tangible evidence to prove she'd been in Barcelona at all and that Nic hadn't lived a dream was the red samba dress, every shoe and scrap of clothing he'd ever gifted her and her black velvet scent on his skin.

Nic stepped out of the glass elevator on the top floor of the Eiffel Tower and walked to the railing, to stare unseeingly at the breathtaking architecture: the Arc de Triomphe, the Champ de Mars—on it went, along with the slow drift of the River Seine, everything that embodied Paris…the city of love.

Knuckles white, he gripped the iron bar as the scathing wind whipped through his hair and pierced his skin with needles of ice. His thick black overcoat with the collar up failed dismally to keep him warm as the shadows of the past had him in a stranglehold.

She'd seen the pictures splashed all over the news. She must have. All the damning articles about his upcoming marriage. A marriage he hadn't even fully committed to. *Yet.* And the way he was feeling right now, Goldsmith could go to hell.

Yeah, right, Nic. You want Santos Diamonds so badly you'd deal with the devil himself.

He squeezed his eyes shut and raked his palm over the hard ridges of his aching stomach, trying to ease the pain of an all-encompassing sadness. One night with Pia and nothing looked the same. Pushing inside her had somehow been the most perfect, most important, most heartbreaking thing he'd ever done.

He'd never pictured a world where his need for revenge would collide with his heart to mingle and smear together, distorting his views, until the future looked vague and devastating.

'Hello, Nicandro.'

His heart stopped.

His first thought: she'd broken her written word. Zeus wasn't coming.

His second thought came hard on the heels of that, because deep down he knew Pia would never break her word. It was sacred to her. So when realisation hit his eyes sprang open to land on her statuesque frame—flaxen hair pinned back, designer powerhouse black suit, long cream cashmere coat, lips coated in armour, eyes glacially cold.

The ice queen was back, and that was more devastating than the implications of what he faced.

Had he been played all along? A first-class double-cross?

Snippets of conversation, visions of business papers and the ultimate feminine power flashed through his mind and, like pieces of a complex conundrum, all slotted into place, fitted together to create a perfect picture of truth.

Dios, he'd been so blind.

The realisation grabbed him by the throat and he found he could barely speak past the iron fist. 'Good evening, Olympia. Or should I say *Zeus*?'

'You may call me anything you desire, Mr Carvalho, while I hear the truth.'

He smiled ruefully as his entire world shifted beneath his feet. 'Is Antonio Merisi dead?'

'Yes, he is.'

Thirteen years. Thirteen years of waiting for his chance to ensure Antonio Merisi felt even a tenth of the pain Nic or his *avô* or indeed his parents had felt gone with three little words and a contingency he'd never have considered in a million years. But why would he have when Zeus's name still lingered on people's lips?

Olympia Merisi. Zeus.

Nic was sure he should feel something. Anger. Rage. Hatred. The need to lash out and scream at the injustice of it all. Except his whole body was devoid of sensation. He was numb. Nic supposed the only saving grace was that the toxic wrangle of emotions Pia had left inside him had been numbed too.

'He died of a heart attack four years ago. I now own and control his companies, as well as my own—and let's not forget Q Virtus.'

Knowing what was coming, he lifted his eyes to hers and locked on to those chips of ice.

'Do I have *you* to thank for the revolt that has brought my club to its knees, Nicandro?'

'Yes.'

'Did *you* manipulate the stocks and shares at Eros International?'

'Yes.'

'Are you trying to annihilate my world, Nicandro?'

'Yes.' No point denying it. Every word was true. 'Except it wasn't *your* world, Pia. Not in my eyes.'

'Oh, but I think it was. You knew I was inextricably linked, regardless. Let's not open the doors to the past just yet. Let us pretend my father is here to answer for his sins. What have *I* ever done to you? What heinous crime could *I* have committed for you to take revenge on my body and on my world?'

'Not you *per se*, Pia. This was not person—'

'Do *not* tell me this was not personal, Nic.' Fire had

obliterated the ice in her eyes until they were a deep violet-blue. 'You made it personal when your mouth touched mine. You made it personal when you held me down and took my body.'

Closing his eyes, he swallowed. Hard. He wanted to deny it, but what good would that do? At the heart of the matter she was right. She was simply laying out the facts in all their stone-cold merciless glory. He could tell her he hadn't known her at the start. He could tell her he'd fought with his conscience. But at the heart of the matter she was still right.

'You're right, of course. The moment I saw you, found out you were his daughter, my mind was set. Destroy him and take from you as he took from me.'

'And what did my father take, Mr Santos?'

'My entire world.'

'Yet here you stand, a new man.'

Right then he realised what she'd said. *Santos*. 'How…?'

'While I was falling into your deceitful practised arms Jovan was digging into your real world. I asked him to check out Santos Diamonds back in Zanzibar. The way you looked at me when I was wearing that necklace…with such vitriol…it wouldn't leave me. Would you believe he actually lied to me too, that day? Something that will take me a long time to get over.'

She'd trusted Jovan implicitly. Had started to trust Nic. Then the bottom had fallen out of her world. So now here she stood, unable to trust a living soul.

The implications of what had happened to her were hitting him as hard as the bullet that had pierced his back all those years ago.

'He said he had no idea what had happened to Santos Diamonds. Turns out he was right there all along.'

Nic frowned deeply. 'At the house? No.' He shook his head vehemently. 'I would have recognised him.'

But would he have? Thirteen years was a long time

to pass without any physical changes. Nic hadn't had the greatest viewpoint of the room back in the Santos mansion, and what was more when they'd met in Zanzibar he'd been too busy fighting Othello's green-eyed monster to see past Jovan's relationship with Pia.

'He was there. He thought you'd died that day.'

Nic thought he'd heard a chink in her icy armour, but when he glanced over she wasn't even looking his way and her cold façade remained unreadable, unreachable. *Dios*, it was heartbreaking. All her laughter, all her smiles, all that fire in her eyes and in her soul gone. Destroyed by him.

Self-loathing sucked his throat dry. When had he become a man he barely recognised? The kind of man who would wreak his revenge on an innocent woman. Had the years of rage and resentment, the obsessive fixation on vengeance, left him so callous, so cold?

'I know my father played dirty with yours. I know your parents died that day, and I am—' Her voice *did* crack then, and he watched her throat convulse. 'Truly sorry for your loss. For all of it. But that's all I know—and considering Jovan was outside until almost the end that's all I ever will know. You have my oath that I will not breathe a word. I only ask that you speak to Jovan for a moment or two. He was under orders to be there and retrieve the debt and I believe what happened has haunted him ever since. He would like to apologise, to explain…'

Her voice didn't just crack—it disintegrated.

And why shouldn't it?

She'd just found out her father had been no more than a greedy, ruthless common crook. A man who'd sent his scapegoats to collect on a bet that he himself had rigged. All because he'd wanted Santos Diamonds. Nic would hazard a guess she didn't even know he'd hailed from the Greek mafia. She was likely standing there wondering if she'd known her father at all. In the space of twenty-four hours Nic had betrayed her, her trust for Jovan had faltered

and her father—the man she'd thought she'd known—had
died another death in her heart. Was it any wonder she was
frozen to the core?

His body flooded with sensation, the agony returning
fifty-fold and he reached for her, cupped her beautiful face.
'Pia. *Bonita*, I am so sor—'

She wrenched away, taking a large step back, and he
watched her blink furiously. 'Please don't touch me. I
don't even know who you are.' She bit down on her lips
and closed those stunning violet-blue eyes for a beat or
three. 'I have no idea who I shared a bed with. What was
deceit and what, if anything, was truth.'

He could taste her misery in his heart and he wanted to
choke on it. Could hardly speak past the lump in his throat.
'Pia…*please*, let me explain.'

'No, I… Jovan is waiting in a black limousine at the base
of the Tower, if you'd like to speak to him, and I sincerely
hope that you find happiness in your…'

Her chest quaked, as if she was holding back a sob, and
it tore at his heart.

Then she whispered, 'Goodbye, Nic.'

Head high, she turned her back on him and walked away.

CHAPTER FOURTEEN

DARKNESS HAD FALLEN over Paris.

Glittering with dazzling promise, lit with elegant flair, the Eiffel Tower stood tall and magnificent, the perfect image from a romantic storybook, ignorant of the fact that Pia's heart had shattered on its top floor.

Suitcases stood by the door of her suite and Pia shoved the last of her business papers into her briefcase and pulled the zipper shut.

If she'd thought the aftershocks of her last affair were bad, they were sugar-coated candy compared to this. This bone-deep sorrow. This heart-wrenching pain. This anger and self-hatred that simply wouldn't cease.

She'd been woefully unprepared for the chaos Nic was capable of unleashing, but as she'd torn down the walls and released all the terrifying implications it had become clear that Q Virtus was no more. Her one promise to her father and she'd failed to keep it.

Pia collapsed on the sofa, surrounded by the caliginous gloom.

Ah, yes, her father. The brilliant and unpredictable scion of a long line of Greek *Godfather*-wannabes. That is, phenomenally wealthy, untouchable criminals.

And she hadn't known a damn thing.

How could that be? Yes, he'd been cold, hard, but she'd honestly thought he'd been honourable at his core. He'd taken her in, saved her life, and she'd spent years desperately trying to repay him and earn his pride. Such an arduous pursuit—because nothing she'd achieved, no amount of money she'd amassed, had been good enough. She'd still felt dirty, tainted. And right now that made her furious. How dared he call her trash when he'd lived such a life? At least she had honour, integrity. Wasn't that worth more than dollar signs?

A hard rap at the door yanked her from her ugly pity-fest and she shoved her arms into her coat, picked up her briefcase and went to catch her flight.

In swung the door and Pia swayed on her feet. Had to do a double-take in case her traitorous imagination had conjured him up from her basest fantasies.

No. He was here. At her door. In all his dark, brooding glory, wearing the same black overcoat and the same depth of pain in his eyes.

He seemed so tired. A profound exhaustion of the soul.

It shattered her heart all over again.

She'd never given a thought to the possibility that Nicandro Carvalho could be so damaged. His polish was usually so brilliant and bright; he shone like a guiding star. But now the gloss was rubbed away it had left something so marred and cold she could plainly see the evidence of his mortality in the rigid lines of his body, and it all made a bittersweet kind of sense.

Pia wanted to take him in her arms, stroke his hair and soothe his pain. A glutton for punishment, clearly. All along she'd been a means to an end. She'd let a man use her, play her, for the second and final time in her life.

Lifting her chin in the face of adversity, she found her voice. 'What are you doing here, Nic? I couldn't possibly have anything else you desire.'

Had he even wanted her in the first place? She had no idea. It had all seemed so real. She still couldn't believe how hard and fast she'd fallen under his spell.

'Can I come in for a few minutes, Pia?'

When she hesitated he begged her with his eyes.

'Please let me speak to you, *querida*. I need to explain. About Goldsmith too—you deserve at least that from me.'

Yes. Yes she did.

Leaving the door open, she walked through to the living area, leaned against the vast plate glass windows and crossed her arms to stop herself from reaching out, begging to be held, for him to take the pain and emptiness away. And what did *that* say about her? Not anything she remotely liked.

Through the shadows she watched him enter the room, his footsteps hesitant, vague, as if he was no longer sure of his place in the world. She guessed that might happen to a man who'd been so driven for thirteen years, only to have the rug pulled from beneath his feet at the final hour.

Pia hated her father right then. For ruining Nic's life. Stealing his parents, his dreams. All she had to do was remember the utter joy on his face at that boutique, playing ball with that gorgeous little boy, and she wanted to cry all over again.

Nic mirrored her position a few feet in front of her and leaned against the table.

'Q Virtus,' he said decisively, and it was the very last thing she'd expected.

'Ah, yes. The rumours leading to its downfall. Mostly true I would say—wouldn't you?'

'Yes, but unless we do something the club will fall. You must know that.'

'Of course I do, Nic. You've made it so that the members no longer trust me—and they have no idea who I even am.'

'Exactly. That's the answer, Pia. You have to show yourself. We need to fix it.'

'*We?*' She laughed bitterly. 'There is no "we", Nicandro, and I can't reveal my identity. I'll lose it all. Then again, what does it matter now? You've already made certain of that.'

The acerbity in her tone made her cringe, because if she was being honest she couldn't blame him. To lose so much all in one night. All because of her father's greed.

'The old rules of the club state that only a Merisi male can lead, and my past is such…' She swallowed past the rise of despair. 'It's dirty—you know that well enough. Listen, I don't blame you for this… Or maybe I do, but I don't hate you for it, or fail to understand your motivation. Nor do I want to see you ever again. So if that's all you came for—'

'Pia, *listen* to me.'

There it was. That commanding Carvalho tone that made her shiver.

'The old rules of the club are archaic—who better to change them than the woman who's made it more success-ful than ever before. *You* are the law, Pia. Change it! Stand in front of them and show yourself. Quash the rumours dead. I guarantee no one in his or her right mind will leave. Worst case scenario: a couple of the troglodytes pack up and go—who cares? I bet you good money that, for some, a woman at the helm they can trust is of far more import than the ghost of a man who is mired in filth.'

'My past isn't much better.'

'*Don't*, Pia.'

His voice turned hard, so dominant her blood fired through her veins.

'Do not lower your worth to his level. I will *not* allow it. Know what I think?'

'I never know what goes on in that head of yours, Nic. You're a closed book.'

'Not any more. Turn any page and I will read you a line.'

'I'm not interested.' *Liar.*

'I think you know you could've approached the mem-bers before now. No doubt you've convinced yourself you aren't good enough. You're ashamed of your past. I think your father made you that way instead of telling you to be proud of the woman you've become and to stand tall before them.'

He was truly intimidating when he was this way—brooding and torrid. Even his body was pulsating, telling her he wasn't in total control and that moreover he couldn't give a stuff.

Frowning deeply, she sifted through his words. Or she would have if he'd given her half a chance.

'Don't you see? That damn hypocrite is still controlling you from the grave. Not only do you work to the extreme, as if you're still trying to prove your worth to him, but you're *hiding*, Pia—behind a curtain of shame. When you're probably one of the richest, most successful women in the world.'

Stunned, she blinked over and over. He was right. She never stopped, was always working, and no matter her success it was never enough. Not for her. Why couldn't she just be proud of herself? Forget the past and move on?

'You brought the female members in, didn't you?' he asked, yanking her from her musings.

'Yes. I was trying to drag the place into the twenty-first century. But to say it hasn't been easy is an understatement.'

'It would be if you were a visible power to contend with. You have more strength and honour than most of the men I know. How you run the companies, the club...I have no idea, Pia.' He moved a little closer, out of the shadows and no one could miss the awe written over his face. 'I am so proud of you.'

Oh, God. 'Don't say that,' she said brokenly. *Don't make me think you care. Not again. I can't take it.*

Nic took another step towards her, reached up and cupped her face in his hands. Hands that weren't quite steady as he stroked over her cheeks with the pads of his thumbs.

'Nothing of what I felt about you, how I wanted you,

was a lie. I've never wanted any woman the way I crave you, Pia, and that is the truth. I never want you to believe you were nothing to me. *Ever*.'

Pia caught herself nuzzling into his hand, so skin-hungry, so desperate for his touch, so dangerously wanting to believe him. To trust in the sincerity darkening his eyes. And it was more than she could bear, because distrust lingered as if hope had been violated beyond repair.

'I think you should go.' She tried to steel her voice but heard the deep shift of higher emotion and knew he'd heard it too.

Leave. Please. Just walk away. Her heart was breaking. Why did she have to fall for a man who'd used her every step of the way? Who was apparently marrying another woman in ten days?

'Pia…' He softly kissed her temple, her cheek, and when he pulled back and looked down at her she felt the agony and torment in his expression in her own soul.

Suddenly words were spilling, tumbling, pouring from her mouth. 'I'm sorry you lost your parents that way. I'm sorry your dreams were stolen in the night. I'm sorry he destroyed that life. But I'm glad—*so* glad—you found the strength to stand tall and make another.'

Tears filled his eyes, pooling precariously. 'Pia…'

'Go. Marry your sweet bride. Be happy. As I will be.'

He jerked back as if she'd struck him and thrust his hands into his hair, ravaging the sexy mess. 'I haven't agreed to marry her! *Dios*, Pia. I wouldn't have slept with you if I had! I made Goldsmith retract the statement and say we were in talks, which is the truth.'

She had seen that, but reading it and hearing it from his lips were two entirely different things.

'Talks? A merger? Do you really want something so cold?' It didn't suit him at all. Didn't make sense. Unless… 'Do you love her?' It came out as a whisper, because even asking him hurt so badly.

Then. *Then* she knew. And emerging into the reality that she'd fallen madly in love with him was as stark and cold as being born, leaving her naked and shivering and utterly defenceless. How could she have been so stupid?

'No, I don't love her, Pia. Which is the entire point. I want Santos Diamonds for my grandfather—before I lose him too. I promised him.'

Pia frowned, trying to piece together what he was saying, but before she even had a chance to open her mouth and ask what the hell he was talking about he flung his arms in the air with all that Brazilian flair and passion she loved so much.

'And dammit, I don't want to feel like this!'

'This?' God, the look in his eyes. Torment. Utter torment.

'This…this *agony* when I look at you! This obsession to hold you in my arms. This craving to have you *now*. Like you are air and I can't breathe without you. This unnatural possessiveness that grabs me by the throat and makes my heart want to explode every time I touch you, kiss you, see your smile, hear your laugh and know it will be over any minute now.'

Her heart was beating so fast she was sure she'd pass out at any moment. Unsure what all that really meant.

He vibrated with a torrid combination of possessiveness, violence, sorrow and an almost desperate hunger. It all worked to pull her into a near fatal frenzy as the end of their game came into sight.

'Pia…'

Like a blistering storm he closed the gap between them, thrust his hands into her hair and crashed his mouth over hers, crushing, devouring.

She tried to pull back, she really did, but it was the first time she'd felt anything close to alive since she'd left him.

The salt of his tears exploded on her tongue and in the back of her mind, though she knew he was using her once more in order to feel something other than pain, she let him take and take and take. Bury his sorrow, his anger, deep inside her.

Somehow they made it to the bed, just skin against skin, frantic, desperately trying to soothe. And then he was moving inside her—one minute slow and somehow devout, the next angry and ferocious as he ran through a tumult of emotions and unleashed them all on her body one by one.

Murmurs filled the air—some she could neither hear nor understand, others so heartbreaking she was on the verge of tears.

'It wasn't meant to be this way,' he whispered against her throat, before inhaling her scent deeply.

This wasn't making love or sex; this was Nic ripping her soul out of her body with his goodbye.

'Please tell me I haven't hurt you.'

Then her own tears came, and she clutched him to her so he wouldn't see her own heartache drawing lines down her temples, down her cheeks.

'You haven't hurt me. You could never hurt me,' she breathed, the lies spilling from her as easily as the tears.

'I would die first,' he vowed as his climax raged through his body.

Pia followed him into the light, that supernova burning bright, only for it to flicker and die as if it had never been.

And when she woke he was gone, leaving the cold seeping into her heart once more. Frozen to the core.

CHAPTER FIFTEEN

Avô TAPPED HIM on the shoulder and Nic jolted back to the present. Though he'd swear he could still feel her petal-soft skin, taste her rich, evocative scent on his lips.

He'd hoped the craving would have paled by now, ten days on. Lust could burn—Nic knew that. But he'd never felt it threaten to incinerate every rational part of him. Obliterate all the careful shields he'd built to make him a functioning member of society, leaving this savage, beastly Neanderthal filled with need and want.

He spun round and thrust a glass of cognac to Matteo Santos, all the while drinking his own in one powerful mind-numbing shot.

'There is a parcel here for you—just arrived. Open it.'

Nic didn't even glance towards the antique monstrosity of a table in Goldsmith's study. 'No. Let Eloisa open the gifts.' Women liked that kind of thing, and she'd made no bones about the fact that wealth and security were her reasons for marrying him. Nic wasn't interested.

He watched the marquee rise up beyond the leaded windows and for the first time wondered what kind of husband he would be.

Fair? Definitely. Supportive? He'd try his very best. Loving? Honourable? Was it faithful to marry one woman and dream of another? The woman who'd left him suffocating in the smouldering ashes of an incomprehensible wanting. It struck him as a kind of cheating all on its own.

'It is not a wedding gift.'

'Have you suddenly developed psychic abilities, Avô?' He was being as facetious as hell today, but he knew what was coming. Knew he couldn't avoid it any longer. Not when Avô had finally cornered him in the same room.

One grey eyebrow arched. Dark brown eyes glittered with annoyance. 'You are not too old for me to whip your hide, boy.'

As if. Matteo Santos had never done so much as flick his ear.

'I want to know what the blazes we are doing here, because from where I'm standing you look like you have another gun to your head—and I am getting too damn old and cantankerous to pick you up again.'

'I did not ask you to pick me up last time.' Even as he said it he cringed with self-disgust at the disrespect and ingratitude of those words. But, *Dios*, he was dying here. Dying as conflict and turmoil roiled in the darkness of his mind. Spectres of anger and regret were circling like vultures, ready to feed off his soul.

'No, I damned well *made* you. Told you to get up and walk again and not let the bastards win. Told you to find something to live for—'

'And I did.'

'Yes.'

He gave a bitter laugh that raked over Nic's skin like the claws of a feral cat.

'Revenge. I know fine well what drives you, my boy. Always have. And I let you, probably even encouraged it, just so you'd take one step, then two. Then four, then ten.'

Avô's voice cracked and Nic felt it in his bones.

'Just so you'd eat and sleep and wake. So I would not lose you too.'

The old man's eyes started filling up and Nic's heart lurched—the first movement it had made, its first sign of life since he'd left Pia, beautiful and warm and safe in her bed.

'And I am grateful, Avô,' he said brokenly.

'Are you really?' he demanded. 'Because from where I'm standing you're just choosing a different kind of death. A longer torture and a slower suffering. You may as well have died on that floor with my glorious girl and her useless husband.'

One fat tear trickled down Avô's cheek and it broke the dam inside him.

His voice was so thick with pent-up emotion it shook, barely audible even to his own ears. 'I only wanted to give you back what you lost. Santos Diamonds. The lost Santos Empire.'

'Excuses.'

White-hot anger filled him. 'No!'

'Yes! You are *not* your father!'

Nic braced his weight off the stained glass windows and blasted the weather pundits who had lyricised for days about this perfect sun-drenched day, clear and calm and hot enough to fry *huevos* on the pavements. Instead the sky was a bruised swirl of black and grey, the atmosphere sharp with chaos as storm clouds thundered across the New York skyline like the wrath of the gods, ready to beat him with their displeasure.

'I don't want to discuss my father,' he said, loath even to think of that day.

'Maybe I do.'

'Please don't,' Nic begged. *Not now. Not today.*

'I lost my daughter, Nicandro, and you can't get her back. And if you do this I will have lost you too. You really think money and diamonds can redeem souls, mend hearts, replace love?'

Nic's mind gingerly touched the words.

Love? Was love like being in the rapture of heaven and

the torture of hell? No. Love was surely sweet and kind. Not possessive and obsessive madness. Unnatural.

The scepticism in his mind masqueraded as logic and argued vehemently with him.

Being with Pia in Barcelona hadn't felt unnatural. It had felt right. Heart-stoppingly perfect. It was when he was without her that it all went to hell.

Pia...

Her name spun inside him like a key tumbling a lock. Even his skin remembered her touch—like a kiss from a ghost.

Was it possible that he'd just walked away from the only woman he could ever truly love? And was Santos Diamonds worth giving her up for?

'No, I tell you!' Avô hollered across the oppressive stately room. 'It's impossible. So I ask you again—what are we doing here?'

'Goldsmith owns Santos Diamonds and his daughter is a suitable wife.' He sounded like an automated message.

'For many, I am sure. For you? Poppycock! As for Santos Diamonds—who cares? Let it go. You either continue to live in the shadows of the past or you break into a new dawn.'

Nic squeezed his eyes shut and bowed his head.

It suddenly became glaringly obvious that he was clinging to Santos Diamonds like a life raft, still desperately trying to reach the end game he'd worked so hard for. Because otherwise it would have all been for nothing and what did he have left?

Pia...you could have a lifetime of Pia, a little voice whispered. Taunting. Teasing. Coercing his heart to beat again. *If* she'd even consider having him after what he'd done to her. He still couldn't believe he'd taken her like an animal in Paris. He wouldn't be surprised if she never wanted to speak to him again.

'I'm scared,' Nic said, unable to let go of the possibility

he would some day turn into the man his father had become in the end. A monster.

'The other side of fear is freedom, my boy. Only when we are no longer afraid do we begin to live. This is your chance for true happiness. Let me see you happy before I go. Knowing there is someone in the world you cannot bear to lose and that you are not spending every single moment holding her to your heart is an unthinkable tragedy.'

Pia stood in front of the double doors leading to the boardroom, thinking how apt it was that she'd been living—*hiding*—in this darkness for so long.

Q Virtus members were gathered around the seventy-foot conference table. One chair was vacant and for that she was grateful. She was unsure if she would have had the strength to do this if Nic had been here. This morning the front-page headlines had been dominated by photographs of the happy couple at a gala dinner last weekend. They'd looked sweet together, she thought begrudgingly.

She should hate him for dredging up all of her loneliness and rage and feelings of worthlessness. For giving her hope of an unconditional love from someone who accepted her for who she was and where she'd come from. But the fact was, how could he ever love her? She had no breeding, like his wife. Her own father had ruined his family. Nic would never look at her with adoration—only resentment for the power of his desire for her. He'd made that clear in Paris.

And he must care for this woman he was marrying, Pia thought, to go ahead even after she'd sent him the package. It had taken her days, fighting with her conscience and her heart, to make a decision. Her head had told her to let him rot in a miserable marriage that was nothing more than a con. While her heart had loathed the fact that her father's actions had placed him at the altar to start with. In the end her heart had won out and she'd gone to visit his grandfather.

Pia couldn't help but smile at the memory.

Striking even in his seventies, the silver-tongued devil had trounced her at Gin Rummy, told her she had 'spunk' and kissed her goodbye. It would be very easy to love a man like that. More so because of his absolute devotion to Nic. He'd hugged her long and hard with tears in his eyes when she'd lifted her necklace—the Santos Diamonds—from the velvet cushion and given them to him.

The only gift her father had ever given her. Going in there, she'd thought it would wrench her apart to give them up. But it had felt so right—like fate. As if somehow she'd been led—by Nic—to this man to return his legacy and make good on the sins of the past.

Then he'd winked at her when she'd given him a note for Nic. One she'd rewritten over and over to make sure that no emotion lay between the lines. That her love didn't pour from the page. Telling him to ask Goldsmith exactly how much stock he owned in Santos Diamonds.

So as far as she was concerned the past had been put to rights. Now it was time to make good on the future. If Nic had given her anything it was the strength to do this. To be proud of the woman she'd become and stand tall before them.

Chin up, she took a deep breath, then another, trying to fight past the anxiety flurrying inside her as she walked down the hallway, concealed by the shadows. Then the double doors slowly opened before her, luring her forward, guiding her into the light.

Stunned gasps were a susurrus around her head and Pia could hear their surprise, feel their shock. This was tantamount to a revolution. This was their new beginning. And hers too. No more hiding. She'd blasted Nic for his dishonesty, his betrayal, but hadn't she too used subterfuge and chicanery to run this club? Yes, she had.

And now she wanted to draw off this last veil—to bring her whole self to the stage. She didn't want to be Olympia

Merisi, the tainted girl who had been groomed into the son her father had never had. She didn't want to sit in her ivory tower behind a curtain of shame and hide any longer. *And if the club falls?* whispered the little devil on her shoulder. Then she'd have done her utmost to be honest and true to them and to herself, and that was more important than upholding a vow to a man who'd thought nothing of destroying a family to fuel his greed.

Yes, despite everything she'd loved her father. He'd saved her, given her a future, but surely after twelve years her debt had been repaid.

This was for Pia.

She stood in front of a high-backed leather chair—a ludicrous throne she'd toss out at the first opportunity. She wouldn't lord it over anyone. In this room they were equals.

'Good evening, ladies and gentlemen,' she said, her voice strong enough to carry through the room as she looked every single man and woman in the eye, her heart steadying as her inner strength bolstered her will. 'I am Zeus. And I believe we have business to discuss.'

She hadn't seen him. Wouldn't even glance at his empty chair—a chair he'd asked Narciso and Ryzard to leave empty so as not to distract her. And Pia certainly didn't need to borrow his courage, even though he'd gladly give it for eternity, because she had the strength of a lioness all on her own.

What she needed was to be loved. Adored. Cared for and cosseted in the way only a lover could. She needed to laugh and smile, have piggybacks and wear jeans, go dancing and give Nic the power to make her feel alive. She needed *him*. Nic just had to convince her of that.

When he'd walked away from his shambles of a wedding all at once he'd wanted an entire future with her—afraid of nothing, side by side, walking into a new dawn to live their dreams. He wanted them fused and naked and damp between his sheets. And in the morning he wanted to kiss that face, cherish all that heart-stopping endearing beauty so tenderly she wouldn't wake, only turn to seek his lips, trusting him, loving him.

That was what he wanted. That was what he was here to beg for.

Nic watched her work the room, brewing and stirring the crowd like a cauldron until magic bubbled in the air. She declared the old laws null and void in this age of a new day, when women were becoming more powerful in their own right and could bring much to Q Virtus. She mentioned Ryzard's wife, Tiffany, who sat straight and tall beside her husband, a look of shock and awe on her face.

And she wasn't the only one. Every man in the room couldn't take his eyes off her, mesmerised by the power, the determination emanating from her. He only hoped to God *he* was the only one seriously turned on, because he had more important things to do than warn off suitors tonight. *Jealous, Nic?* Yeah, what if he was? Nic was his own man, comfortable in his own skin, and that would never change.

In a move that was simply genius, instead of leaving the way she'd come, exerting her influence and power, Pia made her way around to shake hands. One man. One woman. Equals in every aspect. A show of trust that no matter what had gone before her reign she would run the club with honour and integrity.

From the ashes of despair and the flames of fiasco she rose like a phoenix, and his chest felt crushed by the weight of his pride and love for her.

When the doors finally closed behind her she didn't look up to where he now leaned against the conference table, wood cutting into the base of his spine, aiming for a sexy, insouciant pose and royally messing it up by having a seriously bad case of the shakes.

Nic crossed his arms. To stop himself trembling or pulling her into his arms and demanding a second chance he wasn't sure. But if he had any sense—debatable, considering he'd just come from his own abandoned wedding—he would use a gentle hand to coax and lure.

His resolve was shattered when she slumped against the door, clearly fighting the urge to crash to the floor. But she wouldn't. He knew it.

'You were magnificent, *querida*.'

Up came her head, so quickly it smacked off the door— *ouch*. Then down she went, landing on her lush bottom with a soft thump.

Nic had to grit his teeth against the overpowering compulsion to grin at the effect he had on her, thanking his lucky stars it wasn't one-sided.

'What…what are you doing *here*?' she said, the snippy emphasis on 'here' accompanied by a messy arms-and-legs scramble to her feet.

Nic pushed off the table, let his arms fall to his sides and compared his nervous terror to the day he'd clambered from his bed, glaring at the rails that would teach him to walk again as if they were the devil's pitchforks and taking his very first step. He actually thought this was worse.

'Shouldn't you be…?' She wafted her hand around as if searching for the right words as she clung to the wall and walked around the boardroom, getting as far away from him as she could. 'On your honeymoon? In bed with your wife?'

Barely, he stifled the impulse to run over there and grab her. *Dios*, she was so beautiful she made him ache. 'Where are you going?'

'As far away from *you* as I can get. Are you going to answer my question?'

'People only tend to go on honeymoons when they're married, Pia.'

That stopped her. Barnacle-like, she clutched the hardwood panelling at her back.

And he'd had enough.

Nic strode forward purposefully.

'Stay right where you are, *Lobisomem*.'

'No.' He growled in frustration when she stepped forward and started to skirt around the table—on the opposite side to him. 'I'm going to spank you for that.'

'I'd love to see you try.'

He laughed wickedly and darted to the left.

Pia darted to the right and he growled again.

'Now, now, Nic—be serious.'

'Worried, *querida*?'

'Yes. I mean no. Stay back!'

'Lesson number one,' he said, lowering his voice to a commanding tone that he knew would make her shudder from top to toe. 'You are not the boss of me, Olympia Merisi, and when I tell you to stop, you stop.'

She sneered but it was a dire effort. 'Not in this lifetime. Now, run along to your bride and leave me be!'

'*Dios*, I have no bride!' Not yet, anyway.

'Oh? Realised she was marrying a wolf in sheep's clothing, did she?'

'No, she found out I was in love with someone else.'

'What? Who told her that?'

'I did.'

She blinked the confusion from her violet-blue gaze. 'Oh, I see. When you got my note and realised it was all a con you had to get out of it, right? Poor woman—you probably broke her heart.'

'I did not break her heart! Love was never in the equation. I— Wait a minute. Note? What note? And what do you mean *con*?'

She pursed those lush lips. 'You didn't receive my note this morning?'

'No. You wrote to me, Pia? What did it say? Tell me,' he ordered, his agitation at her avoidance ratcheting into the red zone.

Slowly she shook her blonde head. 'I don't think I will. Not until you tell me why you're here.'

His patience snapped and he launched himself atop the table, skidding over the highly polished surface on his backside and landing in front of her wide-eyed and stupefyingly beautiful face.

Then he backed her up until she slammed into the wall.

'Ah, this is much better. You know I prefer the personal touch.' Palms flat to the wall either side of her head, he buried his face in her neck and inhaled deeply.

Gracie de Deus. Finally.

Pia wriggled and pushed at his chest—quite hard, actually. Not that it moved him. They both knew it was a half-hearted effort. 'Why…why didn't you get married?'

Nic straightened up and cupped her jaw, dropping a tender kiss on her temple. 'Because one day I met an amazing woman I intended to wreak the ultimate revenge upon and she was unlike anything I'd ever known or seen before in my life. She scared me, and I'm a man who doesn't handle fear well, Pia. I told myself she was a means to an end and that I'd seduce her into my bed to reach my end game. What I wouldn't admit, even to myself, was that she was slowly stealing my heart.'

'She was?' Pia breathed.

He dropped another kiss on the tip of her nose. '*Sim*. Minute by minute. Hour by hour. Day by day. Until I didn't know what was up or down. Until every breath I took was for her.'

She gazed up at him with a little pleat in her brow. 'Then why…?'

'Why did I leave you lying in your bed while my heart was breaking?'

'Yes.'

'Because I didn't want the same kind of marriage as my parents. My father was obsessed with my mother. Possessive beyond control. My father fired the first shot in that room, Pia. He killed my mother.'

Shock flared in her eyes. 'Oh, my God.'

'My father lost Santos in a rigged deal at Q Virtus—you know that bit. But what you probably don't know is that it was my mother's money—my mother was the Santos heir. My father even had to change his surname to take control. Which he did without question, because he was obsessed with her. But it was an unhealthy kind of love. He often stalked her when she went out. Flew into jealous rages when they got home if she'd even spoken to another man while they were out together. Screaming matches would last for hours. He even locked her in the attic once so she couldn't go out. But the more he pushed her the more she rebelled—and let me tell you she was a reckless, zesty woman to start with. So volatile, Pia. All of it...'

'Sounds like my childhood,' she said, her gaze dropping to the open collar of his black shirt. 'Volatile.'

'I know, *bonita*,' he said, curling one hand around her nape and holding her close for a long. precious moment. 'Is your mother still alive?'

'No, she died of a drug overdose a couple of years ago. I never saw her again after she left me outside my father's house. He gave her fifty thousand dollars to disappear and in a way I felt as if I owed him.'

Nic could hear the pain of being abandoned and the sorrow in her voice at what might have been if her mother had been a different kind of woman.

'I take it your father never married her?'

Pia shook her head.

'Once a Santos marries that's it. Stuck for life. Which was the problem with my mother and father. There's a myth—a legend based around the necklace. The Heart of the Storm. It says only a true intended Santos can wear the jewels or provoke the wrath of the gods. Same if a Santos union is broken. Superstitious nonsense—that was my

retort. But the moment I saw them around your neck…
Looking back, a tiny part of me—one I had no intention
of acknowledging—had always known you were meant for
me, and I think they led me to you, Pia.'

Lips curved, she beamed up at him and his heart flip-
flopped.

'I think there was more than revenge on your mind back
then, Nic.'

'Yes, I know. Our fathers have a lot to answer for.'

Cinching her waist, he lifted her up and carried her to
a high-backed leather chair, where he sat with Pia straddling his lap. Then he tucked a stray lock of hair behind
her ear and went on.

'When my father lost the empire to your father and
Merisi's men came to take ownership of the mansion—the
necklace—my parents had a huge showdown. I walked in
and didn't know what the hell was going on, but my father
was getting more and more agitated. My mother was yelling, screaming that this was it, she'd had enough, she was
leaving him…' Nic closed his eyes, reliving the memory.
'He snatched the gun out of the pocket of one of Merisi's
men, turned and just…shot her in the heart. Right there in
front of me. Next thing bullets were flying, the room was
steeped in panic, and one of the henchmen killed him. I got
caught in the middle of it all. One bullet in the back and it
took me over a year to walk again.'

'Oh, Nic, I'm so sorry.'

'I needed something to live for, Pia. Finding your father,
making him pay for rigging that deal, for sending thugs
to my home to threaten our lives and pushing my father
to the brink… As far as I was concerned Antonio Merisi
had put the gun in his hand and virtually pulled the trigger.
Revenge was all I had to live for. And after that I wanted
Santos Diamonds. That was all I had to live for. Until you.'

'I wish you'd trusted me—told me all this. Now I understand why you'd marry her.'

'I just didn't want that kind of erratic marriage. Gold-smith's daughter is nice…timid; there'd have been no jealousy, no furious outbursts of possessiveness to shake the foundations of our home. No insanity to take one of our lives. But I was missing something in all this. I'm not my father. I am nothing like him.'

'No, you're not.'

'I am my own man.'

'Yes, you are.'

'And you—you are not my mother. Don't get me wrong, I adored the woman, but to marry a woman like her…?' He shuddered.

Pia smiled and shook her head in that way she did—as if he was past help. Where she was concerned, he was.

'But you know the downsides of a safe marriage, Pia? No passion, no adoration. No heart banging with one look. None of that weird bird-flapping in my chest. No violent tug when you're near that changes into a harrowing emptiness when you're gone, as if you're the other half of my soul. *Dios,* I was so proud of you tonight.' He wrapped her hands in his larger palms and kissed her thumb, her knuckle, stroked her hands over his cheeks, craving her touch all over his body. 'I've missed you so much, Pia. Felt I was dying without you.'

'I've missed you too,' she said, the words tremulous and watery as she leaned in to kiss him. Long and slow and deep.

Nic struggled to come up for air. 'That will be enough for me. Maybe you'll grow to feel more when I've gained your trust again, and I'll be grateful for that.'

'And maybe I've loved you from the start.'

He'd swear his heart paused in that moment. 'Maybe or definitely?'

'*Definitely*, definitely.'

Nic grinned as that heart of his floated to the ceiling. There was a God after all—

Hold on a minute…

'And yet,' he growled, suddenly annoyed with her, 'you were willing to let me marry another woman?'

She arched one eyebrow and gave him a load of sass. 'I gave you a choice. Something *I've* never truly had. Until tonight. Until I chose to come out of hiding. To stop living in my father's shadow. Just like you told me to. Ever since he died I've honestly thought I was free. Controlling my own life for the first time ever. But, like you said, he was still controlling me from the grave. I was still carrying the stigma of my past when instead of being ashamed I should've been even prouder of myself for what I've achieved. For coming so far.'

'Damn right you should.'

She leaned forward until the tips of their noses rubbed in an Eskimo kiss. 'You whirled into my life like a hurricane and showed me a taste of life outside the cage I was living in. Just the thought of stepping back into the darkness was more frightening than going forward into the light. So I decided that I'd give you all the facts and the choice was yours to make.'

'What facts?'

'That Goldsmith was trying to pull the wool over your eyes. He only owns forty-two per cent of Santos, Nic.'

'*What?* That dirty louse! I *will* flatten his unfortunate beak of a nose after all. That— Hang on—who owns the remaining shares?'

Her satisfied smile made her eyes sparkle. 'You do.'

'I think I would know this, *querida.*'

'Only if your grandfather told you that I signed my shares—my fifty-eight per cent—over to you at eight this morning. Santos Diamonds is back where it belongs. I gave him the necklace too—laid it right in the palm of his hand.'

Blinking, jaw slack, he stared at her until her words stopped caroming around his head like pinballs and he let them compute. Then she blurred in front of him. 'I don't believe it. You *love* me. To do that you must love me.'

She held his face and kissed away the tear that slipped down his cheek. 'Of course I do. With all my heart. I'm so surprised you didn't realise about the diamonds. You should know the majority shareholder would always keep possession of the jewels, Nic. Didn't you see that in Zanzibar?'

He shrugged helplessly. 'All I could see was you.'

She let loose a half-laugh, half-cry and wrapped her arms around his shoulders, holding him to her, blissfully tight.

'Marry me, Pia. Please,' he begged.

She squeezed him tighter. 'I'll think about it,' she said.

And while her tone was teasing he knew she was asking for some time. Time to learn how to trust him wholly, completely, and after everything he'd done he couldn't blame her for that. It would be torture, but he'd wait.

'And if I say yes I won't want you to take my name, Nic.'

'There is little chance of that, Pia. You'll be taking mine and there will be no arguments. Our power struggles will begin and end in the bedroom, *bonita*. With me in charge!'

She shut him up with another kiss—this one deep and passionate, messy with emotion and unbearable need— until he reluctantly pulled back to dive into her violet eyes.

'This is going to sound ridiculous, but it has been plaguing me and I…'

'What, *querido*? Tell me.'

'What can I give you, Pia, that you don't already have? That you can't buy for yourself?'

Tenderly, lovingly, she ran her fingers through his hair, brushing it back from his brow. 'Your heart, your gorgeous smile and the way you make me laugh. The way you make love to me. Take control.'

Her voice dropped, sultrier than ever, and she licked across the seam of his lips and undulated over his lap with a sinuous serpentine movement that made him hard in seconds.

'I love it when you make me fly. Only you can do that. Only you can take away the loneliness inside me, and when I sway only you can help me stand tall. Don't you see?' she whispered. 'I need you and I'd give it all up to have you always.'

Nic swallowed thickly. 'You would?'

'In a heartbeat. And maybe…one day…you can give me a baby so I can take her to football matches in my stilettos and shout at the referee.'

Nic cupped her lush backside and grinned. He could see her doing exactly that. 'Don't you mean him?'

She arched one flaxen brow. 'Girls can make excellent football players, Nic. There'll be no inequality in my house.'

'God forbid.'

He cinched her small waist, then smoothed upward to cup her perfect breasts. Where he lingered, toying with her through the layers of silk and lace until she flung her head back and moaned. He wanted rid of her shirt. *Now.*

'I can do all of that, Pia,' he promised, unveiling her pearly skin one button at a time and flexing his hips so she could feel his hard desire.

'Oh, you can?' she said, a little breathless, a whole lot turned on.

'*Sim.* Starting right now. I'm going to make you go supernova.'

'In the boardroom?' she asked, aiming for horrified. The flush in her cheeks ruined it. 'I'll never be able to have a meeting in here again.'

'Well, unless you have a bed upstairs, I'm not moving an inch. Ten days I've been without you. Never again.'

'My penthouse is upstairs. Take me there.'

'Oh, I'll take you, Pia. I'll take you to heaven and back. Then do it all over again. Every day of our lives.'

EPILOGUE

One year later...

'DON'T TELL ME...' Narciso smirked as he glanced up at
the towering white sails that flapped in the breeze as the
super-yacht schooner sliced through the South Pacific.
'Your wife of twenty-four hours *is* Ophion shipping.'

Nic grinned. 'Yep. Nice boat huh?'

'Boat...yeah. It would be very easy to feel emasculated
by her power—good job you're the most self-assured, arrogant ass on the planet.'

'Sure is.' And after the best year of his life he was just
as obsessed, just as madly in love, and it was the most awe-
some feeling in the world.

Narciso caught sight of his huge smile. 'I couldn't be
happier for you, buddy. It's about time she made an honest man out of you.'

Nic curled his thumb and stroked over his thick platinum wedding band, glorying in the fact that he finally had
his ring on her finger.

At first she'd kept him dangling from a great height, but
he'd managed to keep the panic at bay, knowing she needed
time to believe she could trust in his love. Then they'd been
busy juggling corporate balls and building Q Virtus into
the phenomenon it was today. No longer simply a gentlemen's club since Pia's unveiling had lured a multitude of
highly successful businesswomen into its ranks. No longer

steeped in archaic rules and masks of secrecy—at least not inside closed doors. Nic had no doubt the club would go down in history as the most respected of all time. Thanks to Pia and her courageous heart.

So this was the first chance he'd had to insist she became a Santos. Who would have thought the person he'd set out to destroy would become the very reason he lived and breathed?

Which reminded him…

'I believe I owe you something.' Nic delved into the pocket of his sharp black suit, lifted his fist and slowly unfurled his fingers.

One look and Narciso burst out laughing. 'A gold pig. I forgot about that. Well, she certainly brought you to your knees.'

'Who's on their knees?' Pia asked, her arm snaking around his waist as she sneaked up from behind.

Nic nuzzled at the soft skin beneath her ear and inhaled her black velvet scent. 'I will be. Later, *bonita*.' Easing back, before he dragged her below deck to their opulent satin-drenched suite, he took hold of her hand and gave a little tug until she twirled in the air. 'Or should I say Aphrodite?' He whistled long and low, glorying in the soft blush that bloomed in her cheeks.

'If I wasn't married…' Narciso muttered, ribbing him as always.

'I would tie you up below deck,' Nic tossed back. 'And—'

'Hey, that's my job,' Ruby said, joining their little cluster and giving Narciso a soft punch in the gut. 'And you *are* married, mister.'

'Blissfully, madly, deeply, devotedly married.'

Nic didn't miss the way Narciso splayed his hand over the slight swell of Ruby's stomach with an adoring possessive touch.

'Something you want to tell us, there, buddy?'

He winked with devilish satisfaction. 'Twenty-two weeks and counting.'

'Whoa—the next Warlock of Wall Street!'

Backslapping and congratulations lured Ryzard and Tiffany into the mix and the conversation quickly veered into a guessing game of 'Who will our children become?' And since Ryzard's firstborn had already made his introduction to the world Tiffany kicked off. Election-style.

'Early signs indicate Max will be equally predisposed to world domination as his father and grandfather.'

'Ah, yes,' Nic said. 'How is your father liking the White House?'

'More so when he has his grandson in his lap, I think. I'd bet good money that right now Max is crawling over his knee in the Oval Office, or he has the First Lady and her security detail catering to his every whim.'

'That's my boy,' Ryzard quipped, laughing as he tucked Tiffany into his side.

'As for our newlyweds here,' Narciso intoned with a wicked smirk. 'Nic tells me they're planning a football team.'

'What?' Pia spluttered.

Nic did his best to keep a straight face and failed dismally. 'I said no such thing—although it would be fun making one.'

Truth was they'd decided to wait, both of them needing to spend some time just the two of them, but he wasn't blind to the longing in those seductive eyes. She had her heart set on a honeymoon baby, so tonight was the night.

Pia's blush deepened, as if she knew exactly what he was thinking, and he got a smack for his lascivious mind that was basically an excuse for her to feel him up.

'I adore you,' he whispered, kissing the flaxen fall of her hair tucked behind her ear. 'With all my heart.'

'I love you too—so much. Sometimes I'm afraid I'll wake up.'

'No fears, *querida*. I'll always be right here by your side.'

She sought his mouth with her lips and it wasn't until he heard the ladies gasp that he managed to pull away from her addictive taste.

The yacht was manoeuvred into dock and even Nic's eyes widened at the view of the tropical island at dusk, their path lit by flaming torches, wending its way through lush vegetation towards the colossal mansion rising from the earth in palatial splendour.

Ryzard was the first to find his tongue. 'I've never seen anything like it. Welcome to Atlantis.'

Their new venture was based on the lost city—a luxurious ten-star resort steeped in mythology and the latest technology exclusively for members of Q Virtus. Their wedding party was the first to stay, and the yachts lining the harbour told him their guests had already arrived for the reception. Avô and Lily were among them—as healthy and full of life as ever.

Right on time a man with a golden tray appeared and Nic coerced everyone into taking a crystal flute.

Grasping Pia's hand, he raised his glass in a toast. 'To my wife, Mrs Olympia Carvalho Santos, for making me the happiest man alive. And to each and every one of you—thank you for being here to celebrate with us. It's a new dawn, my friends. And I wouldn't want to share it with anyone else.'

A chorus of, 'Hear-hear,' filled the air, and the champagne flowed well into the night as they all danced in their brave new world.

* * * * *

If you enjoyed this book, make sure you've also read the previous two instalments of THE 21ST CENTURY GENTLEMAN'S CLUB, *both already available:*
THE ULTIMATE PLAYBOY *by Maya Blake*
THE ULTIMATE SEDUCTION *by Dani Collins*

HARLEQUIN®
Presents®

Revenge and seduction intertwine...

Harlequin Presents welcomes you to the
world of The Chatsfield:
Synonymous with style, spectacle...and scandal!

SHEIKH'S SCANDAL by *Lucy Monroe* May 2014

PLAYBOY'S LESSON by *Melanie Milburne* June 2014

SOCIALITE'S GAMBLE by *Michelle Conder* July 2014

BILLIONAIRE'S SECRET by *Chantelle Shaw* August 2014

TYCOON'S TEMPTATION by *Trish Morey* September 2014

RIVAL'S CHALLENGE by *Abby Green* October 2014

REBEL'S BARGAIN by *Annie West* November 2014

HEIRESS'S DEFIANCE by *Lynn Raye Harris* December 2014

Step into the gilded world of The Chatsfield!
Where secrets and scandal lurk behind
every door...

Reserve your room!

www.Harlequin.com

HP132492